BYE-BYE, BLUE CREEK

Also by ANDREW SMITH

Grasshopper Jungle
Winger
Stand-Off
100 Sideways Miles
Rabbit & Robot
The Size of the Truth
Exile from Eden

BYE-BYE, BLUE CREEK

ANDREW SMITH

Simon & Schuster Books for Young Readers
NEW YORK   LONDON   TORONTO   SYDNEY   NEW DELHI

SIMON & SCHUSTER BOOKS FOR YOUNG READERS

An imprint of Simon & Schuster Children's Publishing Division

1230 Avenue of the Americas, New York, New York 10020

This book is a work of fiction. Any references to historical events, real people, or real places are used fictitiously. Other names, characters, places, and events are products of the author's imagination, and any resemblance to actual events or places or persons, living or dead, is entirely coincidental.

For information about special discounts for bulk purchases, please contact Simon & Schuster Special Sales at 1-866-506-1949 or business@simonandschuster.com.

The Simon & Schuster Speakers Bureau can bring authors to your live event. For more information or to book an event, contact the Simon & Schuster Speakers Bureau at 1-866-248-3049 or visit our website at www.simonspeakers.com.

Jacket design by Greg Stadnyk

Interior design by Hilary Zarycky

The text for this book was set in Adobe Garamond Pro.

Manufactured in the United States of America

0920 FFG

First Edition

10 9 8 7 6 5 4 3 2 1

Library of Congress Cataloging-in-Publication Data

Names: Smith, Andrew (Andrew Anselmo), 1959- author.

Title: Bye-bye, Blue Creek / Andrew Smith.

Description: First edition. | New York : Simon & Schuster Books for Young Readers, [2020] | Audience: Ages 8–12. | Audience: Grades 4–6. | Summary: Twelve-year-old Sam Abernathy, nervous about leaving Texas soon for an Oregon boarding school, has one last adventure with friends when possible vampires move into the town's haunted house.

Identifiers: LCCN 2020030138 |

ISBN 9781534419582 (hardcover) | ISBN 9781534419605 (ebook)

Subjects: CYAC: Best friends—Fiction. | Friendship—Fiction. | Self-confidence—Fiction. | Haunted houses—Fiction.

Classification: LCC PZ7.S64257 Bye 2020 | DDC [Fic]—dc23

LC record available at https://lccn.loc.gov/2020030138

With gratitude and respect,
for all librarians everywhere

ACKNOWLEDGMENTS

I had to say a lot of good-byes to people and places I love while I was writing this book.

Nobody likes good-byes.

But I'm never reticent when it comes to telling my friends that I love them, and to all those who have supported me with their patience and encouragement, well, you kept me going and I am endlessly grateful. You know who you are.

I nearly had to say good-bye to EVERYTHING, and I wasn't prepared to do that (who ever really is?), so vast heaping piles of thanks and love to my wife, Jocelyn; my son, Trevin; and my daughter, Chiara, who are always there for me. I can't even begin to express how much you mean to me, and how proud I am to have you in my life.

If I had a chance to start all over again, I would choose not to, because life is hard and I got through all that stuff, so who would ever want to do it again? That would be crazy! But, if I did, like Sam Abernathy, I would probably want to be a chef, or definitely a librarian, to whom I have dedicated this book. Everything we know as humans is story; librarians are the guardians of that. What could be more honorable and important than that?

Probably nothing.

But there is something magnificent in having the skill to perfectly poach an egg.

Sometimes even the most capable chefs could use a little nudge here and there. So I feel a tremendous sense of obligation to leave this with a note of gratitude in honoring the person who worked hardest on this book: my editor, Amanda Ramirez. Amanda took on the monumental tasks of: (1) dealing with me, and (2) filling in for the irreplaceable David Gale after his health required him to step away from publishing. I will never forget David Gale and everything he's done for me; his cuspidate sense of humor, his brilliance, and his kindness. No easy task to fill in for a giant like that, but then here was Amanda. Thank you, Amanda. I don't know whom you worked for before David took you on as his assistant, but if anyone can hit the same notes he did, you're the one. This was not an easy book for me to complete in David's absence, and I could not have done it without your patience, skill, and support.

BYE-BYE,
BLUE
CREEK

PART ONE
THE PURDY
HOUSE

ON SAYING GOOD-BYE

No one likes good-byes.

Good-byes are like bad haircuts: it takes time to get over the shock and adjust to the "new you," and it's never a pleasant process.

The short summer before I went away to Pine Mountain Academy[1] seemed to be a long, drawn-out, and awkward good-bye. I had already said good-bye to my friend James Jenkins, who had moved away to Austin during the school year, and now there were all these other things to say good-bye to, lining up like a gauntlet of extended family on a chilly Thanksgiving evening when you're the first one out the door: my friends Karim and Bahar, Lily Putt's Indoor-Outdoor Miniature Golf Course,[2] Mom and Dad, Dylan and Evie, that awful Colonel Jenkins's Diner, Blue Creek,[3] and everything about Texas that

---

[1] Pine Mountain Academy is a private boarding school in Oregon. I won a scholarship to go there, which was something I wanted more than anything else in the world—up until a few weeks before I had to leave, that is.

[2] My family's business.

[3] The town where I grew up, which is in Texas, which is also far away from Oregon.

had grown to be a part of me—right down to the color of the dirt and the smell of the air in April. I had to say good-bye to all of it.

And although going to school at Pine Mountain Academy was the one thing I wanted more than anything else in the world, I also didn't want to leave everything else behind.

It was a real predicament, and I kept telling myself how grown-up all this made me feel, but if this was what being a grown-up was like, you could keep it. Because I didn't know what to do.

I didn't want to say good-bye, but I had already gone too far to change my mind.

Besides, I didn't want people to think I was too anything—too small, too young, too *sensitive*—to do something as daring as leave for boarding school in Oregon (which I already knew was going to be colder, rainier, greener, and lonelier than Texas), even if I would have agreed with anyone who told me those things.

So there I was: stuck.

Stuck and wondering how to manage all those long good-byes.

ANDREW SMITH

ICED TEA NUMBER SEVEN; OR, HERE COME THE SPIDERS AGAIN

Anyone who's ever left home to live all alone for the first time in their life knows exactly what it feels like to have thousands of stampeding spiders in their stomach.

And when you're twelve years old, and small for your age on top of that, the spiders can feel like they're the size of rabbits.

What if I get scared in the middle of the night and there's no one to talk to?

What if I have an attack of claustrophobia?[4]

I didn't tell anyone in my family about how nervous I was. I didn't want them to try to talk me out of going away to boarding school. Because talking me out of it would have been easier than getting a dirty look from Kenny Jenkins at Colonel Jenkins's Diner for ordering a large iced tea *without* sugar in it. And that was very, very easy to do.

There were exactly seventeen days of summer left before

---

[4] I have a very bad case of claustrophobia, on account of my having been trapped in an abandoned well when I was four years old.

my family (which consisted of Mom; Dad; my brother, Dylan; and my sister, Evie) was going to pack me up and make the drive all the way from Blue Creek, Texas, to Pine Mountain, Oregon, where I was going to enroll in high school (at twelve years old, no less) and move into a dormitory full of grown-up boys, and share a room with some stranger who would probably end up tormenting me the way a cat toys with a mouse before eventually murdering it.

Here came the rabbit-size spiders again.

"I'm kind of anxious about starting ninth grade too, Sam," Bahar said.

"But you're fourteen years old. You've already done all the in-between grades," I told her.

In school, I skipped ahead two years—the in-between grades from sixth to eighth. To some people, it was like my life was moving faster. To me, it was like two years of unread pages had been torn from my biography.

Bahar was the cousin of my best friend, Karim. She was one of those rare older kids who was nice to me even when she wasn't *forced* to be polite, and she would always stand up to the pressure that other fourteen-year-olds might put on her for being friends with a smallish boy who was only twelve.

I guess that made us friends too, along with all the other things we had in common.

We had the same taste in tea, for one thing. Bahar liked iced tea with no sugar in it, and I did too, which was why

But I could always listen to sensible and smart things from Bahar, and I would listen to them from Karim, too, if he ever thought of anything that was sensible and smart.

I said, "Anyway, why would you feel anxious about starting school? It's just Blue Creek High, and you'll be around the same kids we've known for pretty much our entire lives."

It was a dead time of day, two thirty in the afternoon, and we were the only ones in Colonel Jenkins's. And without even glancing in his direction, I could tell Kenny Jenkins was impatiently glaring at us, just waiting for us to leave so he could wipe down our booth and start concocting the just-add-water or frozen-food horribleness he served up as his "Early Bird Special."

"Well, I don't know," Bahar said. "It's not going to be the same, you know, with all the pressure to be cool they put on you in high school."

"I may as well give up now, in that case. I'd never be able to do that anyway," I said.

Bahar laughed.

"And we always had so much fun doing things around here, Sam. It's going to be boring without you."

"It's Blue Creek," I said. "It's boring *with* me."

I looked at Bahar, and she was looking at me, so we both looked away really quick and shifted in the tufted vinyl booth, which sounded exactly like a (excuse me)[6] fart, and then Kenny

---

[6] I don't swear unless it can't be avoided, so excuse me for saying "fart."

ANDREW SMITH

Kenny Jenkins had been giving us dirty looks, since he always had to make the drinks up special just for us when we came in.[5] One time Kenny Jenkins said to us (in as disgusted a tone as I'd ever heard him use), "You'd think you kids were from California or something, the way you drink that tea the same way West Coast snobs would. Well, I'm telling you right now: I don't serve *kale* here."

Clearly Kenny Jenkins had no idea just how delicious sautéed kale with garlic, vegetable stock, and red wine vinegar really was.

Bahar and I always met at Colonel Jenkins's for iced tea and dirty looks on Saturday afternoons. Well, not always. This was the seventh time we had; the routine just kind of started one time during the last week of eighth grade when I was walking home from Lily Putt's. And like being nervous about going away to Pine Mountain Academy, I also didn't tell my mom and dad (or Karim) about meeting up with Bahar on Saturdays. Because it didn't really matter, did it?

It wasn't like I had a crush on Bahar.

I'd never had a crush on anyone in my life.

Bahar was always so sensible and smart, in ways my parents weren't. And I usually didn't want to hear sensible or smart things from Mom or Dad, since they always sounded too much like directions I had to follow before taking a test or something.

---

[5] Nobody else in Blue Creek ever did something as non-Texan as ordering not-sweet tea at Colonel Jenkins's.

Jenkins, who had to be accustomed to the noises that came from his booths by now, said, "Hey you kids! No farting in my diner!"[7]

And then I felt so embarrassed for so many reasons, half of which I couldn't even begin to put into words.

But it always made me feel good, how Bahar was so nice to me at times, even though she didn't have to be.

And there were seventeen days to go until I'd be leaving Blue Creek.

That was two more not-sweet iced tea Saturdays.

The spiders were having a field day.

The spiders were never going to say good-bye to me.

[7] Even though he had to have said this at least a million times before, Kenny Jenkins always found it hilarious.

ON CRUSHES, LONELINESS, AND KALE

Someone's got a crush on Bahar. Someone named Sam Abernathy.

James Jenkins's text message chimed and lit up my phone. I thought the sound might wake up Mom and Dad and get me in trouble. But high school kids do that kind of stuff, right? Ugh. My stomach knotted. It was after eleven o'clock, and I was *supposed* to be asleep, even though lately I hadn't been getting the most restful nights' sleep.

I rubbed my eyes and picked up my phone from the nightstand beside my bed.

I clicked it to silent.

SAM: Not me. I don't even know what that is. I don't even know what you're talking about, James.

JAMES: I'm talking about a crush, Sam. That's when you just go around in a state where you can't do anything but wait for the next time you get to see the person you have a crush on. Duh.

ANDREW SMITH

I might explain that James Jenkins probably would have been my best friend if he'd still lived in Blue Creek.

Best friend things are always complex, like crushes, I suppose, even though I definitely *did not* have a crush on Bahar, despite what James was telling me. Or texting me.

James Jenkins had moved away from Blue Creek the previous fall to live with his mother in Austin, leaving his dad behind to run that swill mill of a diner. We had both been in eighth grade together even though at the time I was only eleven and James was fourteen.[8] So we were like a pair of balancing opposites—James was bigger than he was supposed to be as an eighth grader, and I was much smaller than I was supposed to be. But James Jenkins hated football, and he quit to do what he loved most of all, which was dance, and also not living in Blue Creek with his father. And now he was at some big-time summer dance academy in Massachusetts, training with some of the best young dancers in America and getting scouted by universities and theater programs and stuff, because that's how good James Jenkins was.

His mom and my parents had arranged for James to come visit me for a few days next week, just so we could hang out with each other again before I left for Oregon (*spiders started rampaging again*), and before James had to go back to high school in Austin, where he'd be in tenth grade and *not* playing football, which was where James Jenkins belonged.

---

[8] His father, Kenny Jenkins, had purposely held him back a year so James could be a bigger and better football player than any other boy in Blue Creek.

Anyway. I *did not* have a crush on Bahar.

SAM: I do not have a crush on Bahar, James.

JAMES: If you say so. I guess maybe there's something wrong with you then.

SAM: Have YOU ever had a crush on anyone?

JAMES: Miss Van Gelder.

SAM: James Jenkins! Our Spanish teacher???

JAMES: LOL. Yes. 😉

SAM: ¡Increíble! 😮

JAMES: Well she was always so nice and pretty. And she smells like a strawberry fruit roll-up. I wonder if she likes unsweetened iced tea at Colonel Jenkins's LOL. Anyway, I got over it.

SAM: How's dance school going?

JAMES: Don't ask. At least it's finished next week and I can go back home to Texas.

SAM: Why? What's wrong?

JAMES: Everything. I don't think I'm good enough. The other boys here are really good. I mean, they're really good. My feet are so torn up, they made me go see a doctor this afternoon. My entire body hurts. The doctor told me I should quit dancing. I guess that's why I texted you so late. So I could talk to someone. Sorry.

SAM: Are you thinking about quitting?

ANDREW SMITH

JAMES: I don't know.

SAM: I don't think you should quit, James.

JAMES: I just wonder what it would feel like one morning if I could wake up and not hurt so much, and not feel like I'm not good enough to be here, and not have people looking at the food on my plate like I'm a loser for what I eat.

SAM: What DO you eat?

JAMES: I'm not telling you. You'd judge.

SAM: 😂

SAM: You just have one more week. Don't quit. You can make it. Are you learning new stuff about ballet?

JAMES: Learning that I'm not as good as people think I am. Learning that there's this kid from Little Rock named Dante and everyone loves him and he's sixteen and about a hundred times better than me.

SAM: What does Dante eat?

JAMES: Kale, water, and bird food.

SAM: 😂

JAMES: ...

SAM: Mmm. Kale.

And at some point between our texts about Dante from Little Rock, how sore James was, and his insistence that I had a crush on Bahar, I must have fallen asleep, because the next thing I knew, it was three thirty and my phone was under my face, with the last words James had texted on the screen: Well I guess you must be asleep. Good night. I will try to hang in there and keep taping up my feet and stop worrying so much about everything. Talk to you soon. Thanks for listening, Sam.

THE REGULAR PART OF MY BRAIN, AND THE ONLY HAUNTED HOUSE IN BLUE CREEK

"Someone's moving into the old Purdy place."

Karim was out of breath from running to my house, and his eyes were as round as Last Chance peaches. He woke me up by knocking on my window, which was open, like it always is no matter what. In most cases, Karim waking me up would have made me mad (this being summer vacation and all), but *real people* actually moving into the Purdy House, which was Blue Creek's only legitimately haunted house, was arguably worth the abrupt termination of about two hours' sleep and a really involved dream about rosewater cardamom pancakes.

What could these people possibly be thinking?

Also, it's normal for a twelve-year-old boy to have dreams about cooking, right?

I'd found myself questioning nearly everything that had been happening to me—including dreams, which aren't exactly voluntary—ever since Karim and Bahar had assumed the task of teaching me how to not be such a target for the older kids I'd be living with at boarding school starting in just three Saturdays.[9]

For any kid in Blue Creek, stories about the Purdy House were even more terrifying than any story about going away to some rich-kids school in Oregon.

"Go around to the front and let yourself in. I don't think my mom and dad are up yet," I said.

But after the twenty seconds it took Karim to let himself in the front door and make it to my bedroom had passed, Karim's thoughts had diverted from what was undoubtedly the most haunted house in the state of Texas to the subject of what Sam Abernathy was wearing.[10]

"Sam. What are you *wearing*?" Karim asked.

"What do you mean, *what am I wearing*? Pajamas. I was in bed. Sleeping. Which is a normal thing for twelve-year-old boys to do at six fifteen in the morning when it's also summer vacation."

(I did not ask him whether it's normal to dream about making rosewater cardamom pancakes. Also, I found myself wondering if we had rosewater and cardamom in the pantry, it being breakfast time and all, and me being suddenly hungry because nothing tastes quite like cardamom, you know?)

---

[9] And yes, thinking about this sent electricity through the thousands of spiders twitching in my stomach.

[10] I should add that Karim was never a knock-before-entering kind of friend; that's how it was our whole lives. He might just as well have been a silent breeze entering our home on a humid summer morning as far as the rest of my family was concerned, and this was Blue Creek, after all. Nobody locked their doors here, not even the people who lived nearest to the Purdy House, who happened to be Karim and his parents.

ANDREW SMITH

Karim shook his head dismissively. "Look, they're Princess Snugglewarm pajamas. Kids in high school would never wear Princess Snugglewarm pajamas, Sam. I don't think kids in high school even *wear* pajamas to begin with. Do you want to get beat up or something? Nobody wants to get beat up in Princess Snugglewarm pajamas."

It was too early for Karim to be assaulting me with all these implications. First—naturally—of course I did not want to get beaten up. And second, I wasn't going to ask him the obvious question about how if high school kids don't wear pajamas, then what do they wear when they sleep? Besides, Princess Snugglewarm was edgy enough for high school, I thought. She was this super-heroic but super-polite cartoon unicorn who went around goring her enemies through the heart with her unicorn horn (which she'd named Betsy), sometimes for ridiculous reasons like the enemy had cut in line or copied homework, or littered, and stuff like that.

"So what's on *your* pajamas?" I asked.

Karim sighed. "I'm not the one who's twelve and all smart and starting live-in high school in a couple weeks. I'll be twelve right here in seventh grade, not getting beaten up, thank you very much. And besides, it's the Houston Astros."

I was confused. "What's the Houston Astros?"

"On my pajamas."

"Princess Snugglewarm is cooler and edgier than the Houston Astros," I pointed out.

Karim had a look in his eyes that said he was going to start an argument about unicorns versus baseball, but I cut him off before he had the chance to. "So. I thought you woke me up over something to do with the Purdy House, but apparently you felt the urgent need to run over here to talk about our pajamas."

"I'm just worried about whether or not you'll even survive going away to school in Oregon all by yourself, Sam. But pajamas aside, dude, someone is actually moving INto the Purdy House," Karim said.

"Are you sure it wasn't just a dream or something? That house has been empty since before our parents were born."

Karim frowned. "The moving van woke me up. I looked out my window and saw it pulling up the gravel drive through the woods between our houses. Somebody had even opened the gates to the Purdy House."

When Karim said "opened the gates to the Purdy House," his voice dropped to a quavering whisper, the type you'd use when trapped inside a haunted house.

Every kid in Blue Creek had heard the stories about what happens when the Purdy Gates open up. But they were just stories, right?

Karim pulled his phone from the pocket of his shorts, and with his voice still lowered said, "I took some pictures."

I didn't know if I actually wanted to look at Karim's pictures.

There was a low knock at my door, which made me jump.

"Sam? Who are you talking to? Is there someone in your room with you?"

It was my dad.

"Uh—" I was startled, but *not* because I was mentally replaying all the stories I'd heard about the Purdy House.

Karim, always on his toes, recovered first. "Good morning, Mr. Abernathy! I just came over to talk to Sam about his summer reading assignment. I'm reading with him!"

No matter what, whenever Karim talked to grown-ups, he lied. Sometimes his lies were ridiculous too (like him actually reading George Orwell, Aldous Huxley, and Kurt Vonnegut), but he never gave up. I didn't really get it, but Karim always explained it as practice for the "big game," which to Karim meant being in the sixteen- to eighteen-year-old range, when lying to grown-ups would become a survival skill.

But Karim wasn't lying about the fact that I did have a summer reading assignment for Pine Mountain Academy. And I hadn't even started reading my novels yet because I was a little bit intimidated by the fact that the teacher was called "Doctor" something. It was hard enough for me to get used to having MEN for teachers when I got into middle school, but having someone called "Doctor" as a writing teacher was a frightening thing for me to adjust to.

"Oh! Good morning, Karim! Have fun reading, boys!"

Then Dad just went away. We could have been committing murder in there for all he knew, outside of the fact that

I wouldn't ever commit murder, even if Karim wanted me to. But still . . .

Karim began scrolling through photos.

"Here," he said, holding the screen in front of my eyes.

The grown-up part of my brain, which was almost constantly at odds with the regular part of my brain, told me that like most of the other townsfolk in Blue Creek, I had bought into a collective myth that was simply made larger and more irrefutable by the fact that so many people believed in it and retold it, generation after generation; and that the Purdy House was just an old empty house that would now have actual, non-demonic, non-cannibalistic, normal everyday people living inside it.

The regular part of my brain has always been a better arguer, however.

THE WOLF BOY OF JUNO

Everyone in Blue Creek knew the story of Little Charlie, the Wolf Boy of Juno.

The legend that had been passed down told of how Little Charlie, who'd been stolen as a newborn and raised by a pack of desert wolves, was first rescued by a band of outlaws who traded the boy for three bottles of whiskey to some German settlers in the 1880s, who then adopted the untamable Little Charlie out to Ervin and Cecilia Purdy, who were among the first people to establish a home in Blue Creek.

That was the Purdy House, and that was what I was looking at in the photo that lit up the screen of Karim's phone.

By any standards, the picture that Karim had taken just minutes earlier was unremarkable. There was a big eighteen-wheel semi that curled like a comma, hooked around the circular driveway on the other side of the big iron gates with their rust-smeared NO TRESPASSING signs. The trailer was white, its doors opened at the back, and had a cartoon drawing of an inchworm and darkgreen Old English lettering painted along the side that said:

WORMACK MOVING AND STORAGE DON'T MOVE AN INCH! WE'LL DO IT FOR YOU!

And, naturally, on the other side of the unmoving moving truck was the Purdy House, a paint-peeling, rickety old Victorian with lots of pointy things and turrets and small windows, which contributed generously to its creepy reputation.[11]

I was fascinated by the people in Karim's photograph. Two of them—obviously the movers, likely with the last name of Wormack—had their backs turned. They were dressed in blue coveralls and were carrying boxes up the front steps toward the open door, which looked like a hungry pitch-black portal to infinite despair and suffering. And there were two people standing on the front porch, watching the guys in coveralls. I couldn't tell much about the two figures on the porch, whether they were men or women, or how old they were.

"Your new neighbors," I said. "I could cook them a casserole or something, if you want to be nice to them."

Karim said, "No."

It was just as well. Nobody really likes casseroles, anyway.

Well, I mean, I'm sure I could pull one off.

Then Karim took his phone back and enlarged the image

---

[11] The Purdy House was the only Victorian in all of Blue Creek, where the majority of the houses were one-level brick midcentury ranches that had been built atop the foundations of the ghost homes that used to be here when the town was originally constructed.

ANDREW SMITH

with his thumb and first finger, centered the photo, enlarged again, and said, "Because take a look at this, Sam."

Karim had zoomed in on a narrow dark window on the third floor of the Purdy House. And in the grainy pixelation of max-zoom cell phone imagery, we could both make out the faint gray form of a pale little boy who seemed to be staring out through the glass as though he knew Karim had been taking a photograph at that precise moment.

"Oh my gosh. That's freaky," I said, looking away.

"It's the ghost of Little Charlie!" Karim said.

I tried to sound more confident and grown-up than I felt. "No. The people who are moving in probably have kids, Karim. Right? He's just their kid, is all, and he's not just standing up there all alone in that window, staring across like he *knows* you're taking a picture. So he's also not thinking about luring you into the attic and eating you. In which case, it'll be really cool having some new kids around here for a change."

"'Having some new kids.' That's something cannibals would say when they're moving in right next door to me," Karim pointed out. "Sam? Can I stay here at your house for a while?"

"Ha ha," I laughed as though I were trying to make Karim think that his non-joke was just a joke. "But Dylan and my dad don't like the Astros, so you'd probably have to get some new pajamas."

"I have some with Teen Titans on them," Karim said.

And I thought:

Princess Snugglewarm > Teen Titans

Then Dad knocked on my door again, and if it was possible to do such things, Karim and I would have completely jumped out of our skins, just thinking about the ghost of Little Charlie, the fate of the Purdy family, the boy in the window, the horrible attic, and monsters moving into Blue Creek, Texas.

"Hey, you two knuckleheads! Would your summer book club like to have some breakfast?" Dad said.

IN WHICH KARIM GIVES THREE BOOK TALKS

No one could blame Karim for running away from home now that new, creepy, possibly cannibalistic neighbors had moved in next door. And I was willing to do my part by allowing him to stay at my house for a while, just on a wait-and-see-if-his-parents-mysteriously-disappear basis, despite the fact that my dad and brother, Dylan, did not like the Houston Astros, my mother was indifferent to baseball in general, and my sister, Evie, did not like Karim at all.[12]

But that's what friends do, right?

Secretly I was hoping Karim's parents would tell him no, that he could not stay over at my house, because Karim would undoubtedly have to ask permission, and in doing so would come up with some monstrous lie about why it was that he wanted to stay with me for an indefinite period of time. Besides, I always felt bad having friends sleep over because of how I constantly had to keep a window or door, or sometimes

---

[12] Evie doesn't like Karim because she says he has a screechy voice, which is true.

both of them, open, on account of my extreme claustrophobia.

So after breakfast with my dad, and after we'd listened to Karim as he made up horrendous lies about the plots of *Slaughterhouse-Five*,[13] *After Many a Summer Dies the Swan*,[14] and *Animal Farm*,[15] I changed out of my Princess Snugglewarm pajamas and into my regular-Texas-kid shorts and T-shirt, and we stole away to get Bahar, who, at fourteen, was far braver and more sensible than we were, so we could spy on the new neighbors, and maybe catch a glimpse of the ghost of Little Charlie—or whoever that was in Karim's picture—up in the narrow and creepy third-floor window of the haunted Purdy House.

The three of us hid in the shade at the edge of the woods between my house and Karim's, where we watched all morning as the men in the blue coveralls with WORMACK embroidered across their shoulders went back and forth, back and forth, carrying lamps and boxes, and then two-manning the sofas and mattresses, in and out, from the trailer of the moving van to the front doors of the Purdy House.

And we never saw anyone else—not the two people who'd

---

[13] *Slaughterhouse-Five*, according to Karim, was about a gang of Agriculture Department meat inspectors who dreamed of performing as an a cappella boy band on *America's Got Talent*.
[14] Karim said *After Many a Summer Dies the Swan* was where Princess Snugglewarm first appeared, as the victim of an egotistical swan who is a cyberbully—and, by the way, he said, the title spoils everything.
[15] He called *Animal Farm* an unlikely kind of feel-good rom-com about a vegan who wins a vacation to visit a working cattle ranch in Wyoming and goes on to become a national barbecue champion.

ANDREW SMITH

been standing on the porch in Karim's picture, and not the pale, shadowy boy up in the window.

"Let me see your picture again," said Bahar, who was always sensible and scientific.

She fiddled with Karim's phone for a while and then handed it back to him.

Bahar said, "There's definitely people waiting on the porch there. And that *does* look like a little kid standing in the window, which is really creepy. Or it could be just a reflection in the glass or something."

"It can't be a reflection," Karim said. "It was just before sunrise. There was nothing to reflect off of; there was nothing to reflect from."

"Maybe this is like one of those television shows where ghost researchers stay inside a haunted house for a few days recording things and measuring EVPs and stuff," I said.

Bahar immediately dismissed my theory, saying, "They never bring furniture with them on those shows."

And Karim said, "What's an EVP?"

"Electronic voice phenomenon," I said.

Karim held up his hand in a *Halt* gesture. "I don't want to hear anything else about that now, Sam."

"What do we even *know* about the Purdy House?" Bahar said.

"It's haunted," I said.

"Little Charlie ate his parents," Karim added.

"Oh. I heard his parents ate *him*," I said.

"Well, someone got eaten in there. That's got to cause ghosts and disturbances and EVPs and stuff," Karim said.

"See? I bet this is all a bunch of gossipy nonsense," Bahar said.

Gossipy or not, I didn't want to have anything to do with the Purdy House, and I knew Karim was firmly on my side with that—no matter who had gotten eaten.

"Well, there's only one good way to find out the truth," Bahar said.

"I'm sure there are a lot of ways, but I don't really want to find any of it out," I said.

And Karim confirmed what I'd been thinking. "Neither do I," he said.

"Research," Bahar said.

Karim said, "It's summer. We're not allowed to use our brains. It could damage them, Bahar."

I wanted to agree with him, but I had a few novels sitting on the desk in my room that argued otherwise. "I'm allowed. I have to read *three books* in the next two weeks."

And Karim said, "I already told you what they're about, Sam."

"Gee. Um, thanks, Karim."

"I think we need to go to the library," Bahar said.

And I added, "Even if Karim's already read every book in there."

WHAT EVERYONE NEEDS TO KNOW ABOUT THE MONSTER PEOPLE

How could anyone possibly know the extent to which the balance of the universe might have tipped off kilter now that actual (probably) living people had taken residence in the Purdy House?

We watched the movers until they finished and left, but nobody else ever showed up outside. No welcoming committee; no housewarming gifts caravanned by cousins or other distant relatives. And nobody appeared on the other side of the very creepy windows either. It was almost as though the three non-Wormack people in the photograph Karim had taken had simply vaporized into the darkness inside the old house.

Like ghosts.

On the other hand, I thought this was almost like a Princess Snugglewarm adventure. She'd never be afraid of the Purdy House, no matter what horrible things it kept hidden inside.

In the early afternoon, the three of us walked down Pike Street, past my family's miniature golf course and Colonel Jenkins's Diner, as we made our way through the bustling center of town[16] toward whatever lean summer pickings might be available from the Blue Creek Public Library.

"We probably would have been better off just going up to the door, knocking on it, and welcoming the new people to Blue Creek. Maybe Sam could cook them a casserole or something," Bahar said.

"We already thought of that," I said. "Too scary. No one has ever been inside the Purdy Gates for as long as anyone can remember. And these days nobody likes casseroles, anyway."

"I bet you could make a great one," Bahar said.

Naturally, I had to agree with her. And I was already thinking up recipes I might try for a Michelin-star[17] welcome-to-the-neighborhood casserole, except for the whole terrifying haunted house thing. Red flannel hash with beets, fennel, and corned beef sounded like something I would do if it didn't involve stepping foot past those gates with the NO TRESPASSING signs.

And just when we turned the corner from Pike to Central and stood before the glass-and-cinder-block facade of the library, Karim stopped suddenly and said, "What if they're vampires? That's why they never came out after sunrise. That's why they didn't even look out the windows all day long."

---

[16] That's a joke, unless you're measuring the excitement level of grasshoppers and cicadas.
[17] Michelin stars are generally accepted to be the top award a chef can receive. I figured that, in my case, it was only a matter of time.

ANDREW SMITH

Karim, who apparently was a scholar on vampirism, had a look of pride on his face, like he was the only kid in a classroom of dunces who knew the answer to the teacher's question about percentages or the prime meridian or something.

I was impressed by his detective skills, and instinctively felt my hand rubbing the side of my neck, because what if they *were* vampires?

Bahar nodded thoughtfully, even though there was no way I would ever believe that sensible and reasonable Bahar would entertain the possibility of our new neighbors being undead soulless bloodsuckers.

Also, I would have been really scared now if it wasn't daytime, and if my friends weren't there so that we could nervously discount every ridiculous theory and then laugh about it.

Karim took his phone out of his pocket and began typing something into it.

He said, "I'm keeping a list of everything we find out about *those people.*"

And when Karim said "those people," he made it sound like he was talking about bloodthirsty man-eating monsters.

Karim's list looked like this:

What Everyone Needs to Know about the Monster People:

✔ Have not been seen in daylight. May be vampires.

And Bahar added, "You should also put down that they have an ugly lamp made out of a stuffed raccoon."

She was right. I'd seen the movers carrying that lamp into the house earlier.

Karim said, "How do you spell 'raccoon'?"

So Karim's amended list looked like this:

What Everyone Needs to Know about the Monster People:

✔ Have not been seen in daylight. May be vampires.

✔ Have a lamp made out of a dead raccoon.

We split up once we were inside the library. Bahar went to the Special Collections Desk to search through the entire bound set of Blue Creek's weekly local newspaper, the *Hill Country Yodeler*. Karim browsed the nonfiction section, looking through books that offered mostly true accounts of haunted houses, taxidermy, and supernatural activities. And I resisted my urge to look through the Culinary Arts section,[18] because about thirty seconds after we'd gotten inside the library, my attention was kidnapped by the huge wall display near the Teen Zone, featuring the brand-new Princess Snugglewarm graphic novel, which was called *Princess Snugglewarm versus the Charm School Dropouts*.

---

[18] I already knew they didn't have anything contemporary there, and I refused to even look at books like *101 Delicious Ring Mold Dinner Recipes*.

I'd had no idea there was a new Princess Snugglewarm book.

"I had no idea!" my mouth said, involuntarily, and also a little too loud for a library.

"Isn't that cool, Sam? We just got it in on Tuesday!" I felt a hand on my shoulder. The hand was attached to the arm and the rest of the body of Trey Hoskins, the librarian in charge of the Teen Zone, the guy who'd just asked me if I thought Princess Snugglewarm was cool, which, *Duh!*, yes.

Karim, Bahar, and I hung out in the Teen Zone of the library at least twice a week during the summer. There were always fun things to do there, like video game tournaments, or stitching franken-creatures from cut-up parts of discarded plush toys and plastic dolls. There was a bulletin board where people put up notices for part-time work for teens, and a space where kids could post their own résumés if they were looking for jobs. Michael Dolgoff, a kid who went to school with us whose dad ran a business called Fat Mike's Worm Farm, had a colorful flyer up in which he advertised himself as a "bait wrangler," whatever that was. There were pictures of worms and katydids on the ad, and a pale, shirtless Michael Dolgoff standing knee-deep in Blue Creek, holding up a crayfish in each hand. Naturally, I had my own flyer there, advertising catering and fine dining services.

Trey Hoskins was probably the coolest non-kid in Blue Creek. Grown-ups often scowled at him because he looked like he was about sixteen years old, even though he had graduated from librarian college and everything. He had a high level of tolerance for noise (which is probably something all teen librarians need to have), he insisted that all the kids in Blue Creek call him by his first name,[19] and he knew about and read EVERY SINGLE THING that had ever been shelved in the Teen Zone, which, of course, included the Princess Snugglewarm graphic novels. Also, Trey liked to make his hair all kinds of crazy colors. This week, it was a brilliant turquoise.

And I suddenly found myself feeling sad when I realized that I was going to have to say good-bye to the library, the Teen Zone, and to Trey.

"I literally had no idea there was a new one," I kind-of repeated, my eyes wide.

"Yeah. And it's the best one so far! I don't know how anyone can make a murderous unicorn so nice and heroic," Trey said.

"Can I check it out?" I asked.

Trey bit the inside of his lip. "Well, I wasn't going to let any of them go out until after Saturday. The author is coming on Saturday, and we wanted to be able to get all the library copies signed by him."

"A. C. Messer is coming here? To Blue Creek?"

Trey laughed and pointed his pale and spidery librarian finger at the flyer tacked to the Princess Snugglewarm wall. The flyer confirmed that A. C. Messer, the deranged visionary

---

[19] This constantly angered Mrs. Barshaw, the librarian who ran the front desk.

ANDREW SMITH

behind all things Princess Snugglewarm, would be visiting Blue Creek Public Library this coming weekend. I was so excited, I wanted to run through every aisle until I found Karim and Bahar to tell them the thrilling news.

Except neither Karim nor Bahar liked Princess Snugglewarm comics at all.

"Why?" I asked.

Nobody ever came to Blue Creek unless they had to.

A. C. Messer was a hero of mine. He should have been a hero to all kids everywhere. He'd published the first Princess Snugglewarm graphic novel when he was just fifteen years old. The only thing that could make him more heroic would be if he was also a chef, but nothing I'd ever read about him had had anything to do with cooking at all.

"I'll tell you what, Sam. I'll check a copy of *Charm School Dropouts* out to you because I know you're a fast reader," Trey said. "But I'm counting on you, and you have to swear to return it by Saturday morning, before our visit from the author."

"Excuse me, but I never swear, Trey. However, I will promise to bring it back on time, and stay for the visit, too. Thank you so much!"

It was only Sunday, which gave me nearly a week to read the book and still manage to find a way to put off what I was *supposed* to be doing for my new school.

And as soon as I had the book in my hands, I wanted to sit down and start reading immediately.

It was almost as though every thought I'd had about the Purdy House, Little Charlie, who had eaten who, monsters, ghosts and vampires, unsweetened iced tea with Bahar, James Jenkins wanting to drop out of his dance program, and moving away from home had been permanently wiped from my mind.

Except, the spiders started doing laps in my belly again.

THE SCREAMING HOUSE

"No one told me specifically what I was supposed to be looking for," I said. "I'm sorry, guys. I guess I got distracted."

Karim and Bahar were mad at me because the only piece of evidence I'd retrieved from Blue Creek Public Library was the new Princess Snugglewarm book, and it provided no insights as far as the history of the Purdy House or the monstrous kid named Little Charlie were concerned.

The three of us had gone back to Karim's house to "aggregate" (as Bahar called it) the evidence we'd gathered, even though all I had was a real cracker of a story about babysitters who stole things from the houses of their clients and ended up on the business end of Betsy, Princess Snugglewarm's punishing, ice-pick-sharp skull spike.

Karim was only slightly more helpful than Princess Snugglewarm, to be honest. He'd taken out a book that had been published two years before but had never been checked out until today. Karim's book was a scholarly work called *Attachments: The History of Injustice and Its Reported Links to Haunted Places in America*, and it must have weighed fifteen pounds.

"At least there are pictures in it," Karim pointed out.

And I said, "There are pictures in my book too."

Then Karim plopped his ghost book down on the floor between us, fanned it open to about page 400 or something, and poked a finger down in the center of an old black-and-white photograph.

"Bam!" he said. "The Purdy House."

"What does it say about it?" I asked.

Karim shook his head. "I don't know. I didn't read it. The print is really small and there are some words in here I've never heard of before. But at least I found the picture."

Karim spun the book around so that it was facing me. The photograph of the Purdy House must have been taken a long time ago, because the gates were not chained shut, and the NO TRESPASSING signs had not been installed. Other than that, and the fact that the house in the book was not dilapidated and splintering, the Purdy House of the picture was undoubtedly the place that everyone in Blue Creek knew stood right next to Karim's house.

And beneath the photograph was the only entry about the Purdy House in the entire fifteen-pound book. The caption said this:

Purdy House, Blue Creek, Texas: Sometimes referred to as the "Screaming House." It was originally constructed by Ervin Purdy and Cecilia Pixler-Purdy, and reported to have been the

site of numerous disappearances, acts of alleged cannibalism,
and other unexplained disturbances dating back to the late
nineteenth century. The vacant residence has been the site
of several studies, most recently by the University of Arizona,
2002, which provided inconclusive results.

I looked at Karim. "People called it *the Screaming House*?"

"I've never heard it called that before," Bahar said, and she'd probably heard of twice as many things as Karim or I had, easily.

"Obviously my parents didn't do their neighborhood research very well before deciding to move here," Karim said. "But I've never heard the place *scream*."

"Nobody would ever want to live next to a home that actually screams," I said.

Just thinking about what screams from a screaming house would sound like gave me chills, even though it was a hot, sunny, summer day and I was sitting on the floor of Karim's bedroom, looking through books in the company of two of my closest, non-screaming friends.

But it was Bahar, naturally, who'd uncovered the most *real* information on the Purdy House, or at least information that was as real as anything else you'd ever find in the *Hill Country Yodeler*. She'd made three photocopies of an article she'd found in the Special Collections, which dated all the way back to 1919, the first year our local paper went into circulation. The article was about the Purdy House and the unfortunate people who'd lived there, or those who'd only visited it.

And Bahar had brought multiple copies of other articles too, so we could all look at them at the same time. But, Bahar being Bahar, she said we would read them in chronological order, together, and starting with the oldest one. It was pretty interesting, but it also felt a little bit too much like being in school.

I was torn with guilt because all I really wanted to do was finish my Princess Snugglewarm book so that I could give it back to Trey before Saturday and then somehow get on to reading the stack of novels I'd been assigned for my summer schoolwork.

"Let's read this one first," Bahar said. "We'll look at the next ones after we figure out if there's anything of substance that connects the Purdy House of a century ago to the Purdy House of today. Judging from the headlines, there's some stuff in here that I've never heard about."

"I'd never heard about the whole screaming thing to begin with," I said.

So we sat together in Karim's bedroom and read the first article from 1919. It was impressive to me to think about how much Blue Creek had changed in the past century. On the front page of that issue of the *Hill Country Yodeler*, there was a story about how federal law enforcement agents had arrested a group of Communists who'd come from California.

Maybe Blue Creek hadn't changed that much, I thought. At least the agents had been successful at keeping California Communists out of Blue Creek for the next hundred years.

But the first story Bahar wanted us to read was not about Communists from California so much as it was about demons and stuff from the darkest depths of wherever demons and stuff like to come from.[20] And like a lot of newspapers from that era, the *Yodeler* stacked headlines with subtitles over most stories, and the one Bahar gave us to read started off with the following openers:

A HOLY TERROR.
THE HOUSE OF SCREAMS.
A MODEST STORY FROM BLUE CREEK-TOWN.

Last Saturday, the *Hill Country Yodeler* published a remarkable story based on an interview with a rancher from Blue Creek-Town which detailed the frightening goings-on in the abandoned home once belonging to Ervin Purdy and Cecilia Pixler-Purdy.

The story recounted by the rancher, Jacob Swift, was immediately suspect due to Mr. Swift's incarceration for public intoxication and the likelihood that the effects of bug-juice

---

[20] Also, apparently, a hundred years ago Blue Creek was called Blue Creek-Town.

played havoc with liberating hob-goblins from the man's wild imagination. A second source has since come forth, however, so well-vouched-for that we now must accredit Mr. Swift's account a confident degree of credence.

The newly revealed source, a constable from San Jacinto County, confirms the following strange events as fact. We provide his recollection for what it is worth:

Newly arrived in Blue Creek-Town, Constable Peter Frick, who was at the time traveling to Austin, was startled from his sleep in the night where he camped near the Creek by indescribable screams thundering from the north, coming from the direction of the town's settlement.

Mr. Frick arose, but hearing no further sounds and seeing nothing which might alarm him, returned to his bedroll. Shortly afterward the screams came again, with a renewed intensity. Mr. Frick described the sound as something that had convinced him that he had encamped in the path of a cyclone. This time, upon rising, the constable noted a swirling black cloud rising in the north, which blotted out all light from the moon and stars, as though the form itself was quite cohesive and impenetrable.

ANDREW SMITH

Being an agent of the law, Mr. Frick retained his Winchester and followed Blue Creek in the direction of the terrible cacophony, where he soon found himself standing before the locked gates of the Purdy House, from which he determined the screams had been emanating.

At this point, the black cloud which was hovering like a winged guardian above the House began to descend, and Mr. Frick took his rifle and fired twice into the cloud. His description of the experience is very succinct: "The thing was at least twenty feet across, moving like an enormous bird. Once I fired into the demonic form, the being dispersed and vanished, and the screams from within the house, which sounded like all manner of suffering and pain, subsided."

It was only then that Mr. Frick encountered the shaken and senseless Mr. Swift, inebriated and frightened to the point of incoherence, cowering inside the locked gates of the Purdy House.

It was impossible to determine how Mr. Swift had managed to pass beyond the secured gates.

The constable was able to subdue Mr. Swift, who was remanded to the custody of the authority of Blue Creek-Town.

Mr. Frick experienced no further disturbances that night.

Mr. Swift, on the other hand, insisted that he
had been visited upon by the cannibalistic child
named Charlie Purdy, an orphan boy adopted
by Ervin and Cecilia Purdy, who had vanished
without a trace some twenty years earlier.

"Okay. That's pretty weird," I said.

"That's freakin' scary," Karim added.

"No. I actually thought it was weird that a hundred years
ago, the *Yodeler* started out trying to be an actual, real newspaper, as opposed to one that just criticizes the food at the golf
course and posts angry editorials about speeders from Austin,"
I said.

WHAT EVERYONE NEEDS TO KNOW ABOUT THE MONSTER PEOPLE (PART 2)

What Everyone Needs to Know about the Monster People:

✔ Have not been seen in daylight. May be vampires.

✔ Have a lamp made out of a dead raccoon.

✔ Have a hideous black flying beast that is bulletproof and comes out of their house at night during all the screaming.

IN WHICH WE TALK ABOUT PRINCESS SNUGGLEWARM, LOVE, AND THE BEST KIND OF MAYONNAISE

"No one who's actually read a Princess Snugglewarm graphic novel in its entirety could ever possibly resist becoming a completely dedicated subject of her kingdom, or princess-dom, or whatever it's called," I said.

I was lying in bed with the book fanned open on my chest. I'd finished reading *Charm School Dropouts* after dinner, which meant I could probably read it at least five more times before I had to give it back to Trey at the library on Saturday morning.

The house was quiet; Dylan, Evie, and Mom and Dad had all gone to sleep. Karim stood with an arm resting on the sill of my (as usual) open window, with his head turned so one ear was pointing out in the direction of the Screaming House. Just in case. Also, he'd brought his Teen Titans pajamas, which I could have given him a hard time about, but I let it slide.

Regardless: Princess Snugglewarm > Houston Astros > Teen Titans.

"I *have* read one from start to finish," Karim said. "It was the one about the vampire impalas or antelopes, or something."

"Oh! *Princess Snugglewarm versus the Vampalas and Vampelopes*. That was a good one. It had a Gobblepotamus in it too."

I'll be honest: *Princess Snugglewarm versus the Vampalas and Vampelopes* had tested my enduring commitment to Princess Snugglewarm. It's all because in that particular volume, Princess Snugglewarm confessed her deep hatred for mayonnaise. It would be one thing if she had made it specifically clear that *jarred*—or, worse yet, plastic-squeeze-bottle—mayonnaise was disgusting and could possibly turn someone into an eternally undead bloodsucking creature of the savanna, while real, fresh homemade mayonnaise (or, better yet, aioli) was one of the greatest culinary achievements of humankind.

If Princess Snugglewarm only knew!

I had been so disheartened by that particular anti-mayonnaise episode that I'd even written a letter of protest to A. C. Messer, author-illustrator of Princess Snugglewarm, which he'd never answered. And then, by the time the next Princess Snugglewarm graphic novel had come out, which was about a ring of homework cheaters, I had forgotten all my doubts about her magnificence, because who doesn't want to see cheaters who copy homework get gored by a unicorn, right in the middle of math class?

"I don't know. Stabbing people in the heart with Betsy just because they put mayonnaise on cooked macaroni and call it a pasta salad seems a bit rough."

"It won't seem rough fifty years from now when everyone in the world wakes up, Karim," I said. "It just shows how far ahead of her time Princess Snugglewarm really is. And anyway, it was *jarred* mayonnaise. I wrote to the author and asked him if there'd be a follow-up about how handmade mayonnaise is outstanding."

"Did he answer?" Karim asked.

"Well. Not in writing," I said.

Karim nodded and looked out the window. There was nothing to see, and the night was devoid of bloodcurdling screams, or if there were any screams going on, they couldn't be heard over the whirring chorus of cicadas and tree frogs. Karim said, "I broke up with my last *significant other* over mayonnaise, as a matter of fact. Because every time we'd kiss, well, the thought of mayonnaise would just about make me gag. Mouths that touch mayonnaise will never touch mine, Sam."

I should mention here that I have *never* kissed anyone who wasn't my mom or my dad, whether they ate mayonnaise or not, so the thought of kissing someone was terrifying to me and filled me with all kinds of awed respect for Karim, to whom kissing other people was as unremarkable as looking both ways before crossing a street. I didn't get it. And I never wanted to grow up if the toll to get past that particular marker meant kissing someone when you weren't required to, mayonnaise or not.

Also, I should probably explain that for nearly as long as I'd known him, Karim had been a boy who constantly had a steady *significant other*. He had gone out with no fewer than four girls this past school year, and Karim was only just about to start seventh grade. I'd lost track of the most recent significant others after he'd broken up with Hayley Garcia, who'd been president of our middle school Science Club, but I could always tell when Karim was experimenting with his independence, because those were the days when he'd spend more time with me—like now, when he was practically living at my house. And knowing that Karim had broken up with one of his girlfriends over the mere prospect of having to go to a school dance with her made it seem all the more reasonable that he would break up with someone else over an emulsion of egg yolk and oil—mayonnaise.

"So it was mayonnaise that got between you and Hayley Garcia?" I asked.

Karim made a kind of clucking sound. "No. Hayley was a long time ago."[21]

And Karim continued, "I didn't tell you, but I started going out with Brenden Saltarello at the end of April. Brenden puts mayonnaise on everything, even *corn dogs*. Corn dogs. Can you imagine? Putting mayonnaise on a corn dog is like using the flag of Texas to wipe your feet. I stayed over at his house on his thirteenth birthday, and his dad even made a chocolate cake with mayonnaise in it. I just couldn't take it anymore. It was mayonnaise insanity. It was like living on Planet Mayonnaise.

---

[21] To correct the record here, Hayley was only a few months ago.

I still really like Brenden a lot, but I had to break up with him, all entirely due to mayonnaise."

There was suddenly so much I wanted to say to Karim, not the least of which was this: *Chocolate mayonnaise cake is delicious.*

Instead what I said was this: "Wait. *What?*"

I sat up in bed and my library book plopped to the floor.

I wondered if Princess Snugglewarm would be mad at me for that.

Karim looked out the window and shrugged. He said, "Yeah. Mayonnaise broke us up."

"No. I mean, *Brenden Saltarello?*"

Brenden Saltarello was a year older than Karim and I. He was going into eighth grade. Brenden was super-popular and wrote for the school newspaper, the *Mustang*, and he played pitcher on the baseball team. Also, I had seen Brenden wearing a Princess Snugglewarm T-shirt a few times at school last year, which placed him squarely in the "people who are okay as far as I'm concerned" category, so I totally didn't mind if my best friend was going out with him.

"Yeah. Well, sorry I never said anything about it. But you're the first person I told, Sam. I mean besides my mom and dad, and Bahar. It was Brenden who asked me if I wanted to go out with him too, not that it matters. He told me he had a *crush* on me. I never even really thought about it until Brenden asked, but I guess I've also always been kind of interested in going out with boys, too, you know, what that would be like. And Brenden always made me feel like it was no big deal, which it isn't. And then I realized that I liked going out with Brenden more than I ever liked going out with anyone else."

Then Karim looked at me. It was dark, but I could tell by the sound of my friend's voice and the way his eyes changed shape in the charcoal reflection of the night sky that Karim was telling me the truth, and that he was sad about breaking up with Brenden too.

Friends can tell these things about each other.

And I was so confused about this *crush* thing that everyone else apparently knew about, like what it felt like, and how to know if you were having one.

I sighed, thinking about tea with Bahar and not saying anything to anyone.

And Karim added, "We both cried when we decided to split up. But you know—Blue Creek. And, I don't know, the other boys who go out with boys at Dick Dowling, or the girls who go out with girls, they're all way braver than I am. Besides, Brenden plays baseball, and those kids can be . . . well, you know."

I said, "Oh."

Karim just cleared his throat and turned again to look out in the direction of the Purdy House—the Screaming House.

He said, "You're not jealous, are you?"

And I have to say that unlike Karim, I am not a good liar,

and I would especially never lie to my best friend. But I felt confused about so many things.

I said, "Well, I am kind of jealous of Brenden Saltarello because you're my best friend."

"We'll never *not* be best friends, Sam." Then I could hear the smile in Karim's voice when he said, "Besides, long distance relationships never work out, and Oregon's, like, two thousand miles away."

"That's not what I meant."

"I know."

"But it's dumb to break up with someone you really care about over something as unimportant as mayonnaise. Or baseball."

Karim said, "It just . . . No. Gag. And besides, Blue Creek is a town that makes kids be what Blue Creek wants them to be. You know that. That's why you're going to Oregon for high school. It's why James left too. Brenden's going to be a baseball player, or a news reporter in Dallas or something, and I'm just going to be here in Blue Creek, alone, texting you guys who are all so far away."

I'll admit it that I was sad when James left Blue Creek.

The whole town—James's dad especially—wanted James to be a great football player (which he was), but he only wanted to study dance (and he was such a talented dancer, and he loved dancing and hated football, besides). So his mom took him away from Blue Creek, so she could let James be James.

Maybe Karim and Brenden would get their chance too.

It seemed like a couple of minutes passed without Karim and me saying one word to each other. We just listened to the sounds of the insects and the frogs outside in the muggy night.

I said, "Well, I bet you anything it's *jarred* mayonnaise that Brenden always uses. One of these days, I'll make homemade mayonnaise for you. It will change your world, Karim. Maybe you could bring some to Brenden. He'd never eat the jarred kind again. And you'd live happily, and bravely, ever after. The end."

"Thank you, Sam."

"Karim?"

"What?"

"Did Brenden Saltarello ever make fun of you for wearing Teen Titans pajamas?"

"Shut up, Sam."

PART TWO
BORIS

THE KID IN THE WINDOW

Everyone at Lily Putt's Indoor-Outdoor Miniature Golf Course could tell I wasn't focused on my job at all the next day.

My parents owned Lily Putt's Indoor-Outdoor Miniature Golf Course, Blue Creek's version of an amusement park, so I worked there a few days every week. And when I did, I had free rein to customize the menu selections at the snack bar.

Today would be Thai chicken burgers with cucumbers, cilantro, and spicy peanut sauce.

Karim had spent the night, but we hadn't slept at all because we'd stayed up talking about Princess Snugglewarm and Karim's evolving love life, all while trying to listen for the terrifying Purdy House screams, but they hadn't come. Even though it never mattered to my parents when Karim slept over, this time he'd told them it was because his house had a scorpion and kangaroo rat infestation, and there was no telling how long the poison gas used by the exterminator would take to dissipate. He said his parents had flown down to a nudist resort in Cancún for a week and left him with a hundred dollars so that he wouldn't starve to death.

Karim was really working on his lying-to-all-adults A-game.

But it was good for me to talk to Karim all night long about pointlessly random things. The days seemed to be rushing past me, and before I knew it, I'd be packing up and leaving my friends and family behind for months and months, and Karim lulled the spiders in my stomach to a kind of confused quietness, even though just admitting that fired them up again.

So the next day, the day I was working at Lily Putt's, we were supposed to reconvene our three-person inquiry into the history of the Purdy House. To be honest, neither Karim nor I really wanted to read any more articles after the first story about the drunk guy and the sheriff who shot at the monster in the sky. Karim made such a big deal about how scary the story about the screams and the black invisible giant bird monster was, while Bahar remained our steady voice of reason. ("A hundred years ago, people were seriously impressionable, which explains the whole Communists-from-California thing," she'd said.) And as usual, I was caught somewhere between the cousins—wanting to be sensible like Bahar, but feeling a panicked sense of irrational terror, like Karim.

So I kept my three as of yet unopened novels behind the counter at Lily Putt's snack bar, unrealistically thinking that I might have a chance to read something when I wasn't busy, but every time I even considered opening a book, I'd start to nod off because I was so tired from listening for things that weren't there with Karim, who was still at my house, undoubtedly taking a nap in his Teen Titans pajamas, in *my room*, and in the secure safety of the air-conditioned daytime.

It was a miserable and sweltering-hot day, and the Thai chicken burgers ended up being a little more labor intensive than I had anticipated. All I really wanted to do was take a quick nap somewhere that was not in the dark, somewhere not with screaming or swirling black birdlike clouds, and not with the ghost of Little Charlie.

And it was a busy afternoon too.

Whenever school was out in Blue Creek and it was as hot as it gets in Texas in summer, the indoor air-conditioned course regularly filled up with miniature golfers who were almost always hungry, or losing their balls, or needing assistance getting their putters unstuck from the mechanical llama hazard.

Tap tap tap tap tap!

"Hey. Hey. Hey."

I swear (excuse me)[22] that I had only fallen asleep for a few seconds when some little kid started knocking on the glass of the order window. And it was probably a good thing he woke me up, because I was just about to make a deep descent into a paralyzing sweaty-hot midday nightmare, which is the worst, most horrifying type of nightmare a guy can have. This one was like a movie whose opening credits rolled over a shot of the Purdy House gates on a windblown, moonless night.

---

[22] Because, you know, I never swear.

Tap tap tap tap tap! "Hey. Hey. Hey. Is anyone back there? Hey."

I'll admit that I had to stand on top of an overturned plastic milk crate when I took orders, just so that really short people (like the kid who smudged his knuckles all over the order window) wouldn't think they were talking to some disembodied spirit of a child-chef.

My voice crackled with denied sleep. "Yes. Hello! Welcome to Lily Putt's Indoor-Outdoor Miniature Golf Complex," I said.[23]

The kid on the other side of the smudged window looked to be about seven years old, and he had dirty hands, with artificially colored some-type-of-sweet-drink thing staining the skin around his mouth, and little golden crumbs of dried snot[24] ringing his nostrils like they were a pair of tiny bear traps. I could practically smell him through the little sound hole in the order window, and I could only imagine he smelled like an old damp dishrag.

Reading my hand-lettered sign above the glass, he said, "What's a Thai chicken burger?"

He pronounced it "thigh."

I cleared my throat. "A *Thai* chicken burger is seasoned with a bit of green curry and lemongrass, grilled to a hard caramelized sear, and topped with a drizzle of spicy peanut sauce and quick-pickled cucumbers, daikon, and cilantro. We

---

[23] This is what my dad required me to say to every customer. The "complex" part was a new touch. Dad wanted the people of Blue Creek to appreciate the vastness of our family's enterprise.
[24] (excuse me)

ANDREW SMITH

serve it on a soft steamed roll with a side of tempura green bean fries and a mango-chili-lime aioli."

Karim really needed to try this aioli. It would change him forever.

But the kid at the window was unfazed and emotionless. It was almost like I was talking to a cardboard cutout, or our mechanical llama hazard.

"I don't like any of that," he said.

Confident I would send this two-dimensional unpleasant kid away happy one way or another, I said, "We have a money-back guarantee on all our burgers."

The kid was as emotional as a frozen cod. "Keep your money. I hate all of that stuff. Is this a torture chamber or something?"

"Well, we also have regular hot dogs," I said, remaining cheerful and enthusiastic like a good snack bar chef should always be.

"Are they on buns?"

I felt like we were making progress now. "Yes!"

"I don't like buns."

Look, I get it. Even at twelve years old,[25] I understand that sometimes customers just want to feel confident that you're going out of your way to personalize their experience. So I

---

[25] But also, I might add, about to start high school more than a thousand miles away, which made me feel terrifyingly grown-up and wise, except with a stomach full of moshing spiders.

said, "I could just put a plain wiener—assuming you like it cooked—inside a bag of crushed corn chips or something. I really can make anything you'd like."

The kid just stood there, a blank (but dirty) slate for a face, staring at me.

It was almost like he had entered a state of suspended animation or something.

If I wasn't so anxious about his strangeness, I would have probably turned around to make sure the second hand on our clock was still moving.

I waited for him to make up his mind, giving him a wide-eyed, time-frozen, and grinning nod of encouraging patience.

Nothing. Just staring and looking like a creepy little mannequin.

The kid, unblinking, mouth slightly open, glanced back over his shoulder and then turned to me and said, "Have you ever had to hide inside a garbage dumpster to avoid being attacked by mountain lions? I have."

Just the thought of being inside a dumpster made my chest constrict from the anticipation of claustrophobia. But you'd think someone who'd had to hide in a garbage dumpster to avoid being attacked by mountain lions would be more open-minded about food.

"Oh," I said. "For how long?"

"Until trash day."

"I see."

He was staring again, not doing anything else.

After a good half minute, I said, "Chicken nuggets?"

"Do they come with ranch?"

Maybe I had finally cracked the frozen sea of ice between us.

I said, "Yes!"

The kid said, "I already told you once that I don't like chicken. And I don't like ranch, either."

More staring and waiting.

A lot more waiting.

"So then, how about a plain hot dog with no bun?" I asked.

The kid was starting to make me feel so nervous and self-conscious that I was considering breaking into a song and dance for him, but I already guessed that he didn't like music or dancing.

"Do you have those little plastic packets of mustard, ketchup, and relish?"

"Of course we do."

"Sweet or dill relish?"

Ha! He would not be victorious this time, I thought.

"We have both—dill *and* sweet."

He wiped his nose with the back of an index finger.

And I added, "So, if you *relish* the thought of a hot dog, you have come to the right place!"

Sometimes I crack myself up. But the kid was not impressed. Spending days inside a dumpster to avoid being eaten by mountain lions can pretty much ruin the impact of humor for the rest of your life, I thought.

The kid took a deep breath as though he had finally decided on what he wanted, which happened to not be something to eat, as opposed to something that might make me feel bad. He said, "You're not funny, and you're not nice. It must be so exhausting for you, letting people down as much as you do. Does anyone even like you at all?"

Then he walked away without ordering anything.

I'll admit it: for the rest of the day I moped around in a daze, trying to figure out why some random kid had shown up just to let me know about all the things he hated, and how he thought I was a friendless disappointing failure who never had to hide in a dumpster from mountain lions and who nobody could possibly like. And even though he was a complete stranger, someone I'd never seen before and would probably (hopefully) never see again, for some unexplainable reason the kid made me feel completely depressed and inadequate.

If there had been a dumpster nearby, I would have hidden in it.

And since just thinking about hiding in a dumpster makes me anxious, I suppose I'd be lion food.

OF CRUSHES, KILTS, CAMPING, AND LINE DRIVES

One time after unsweetened Saturday tea a few weeks ago, Bahar and I found ourselves walking through Lake Marion Park, which was not the most direct route from Colonel Jenkins's Diner to Bahar's house, but it was a nice day, and she asked if I wanted to go that way.

Let me be clear, that's *not* a crushy thing to do.

Right?

Everyone in Blue Creek went to Lake Marion Park, even people who I'm sure didn't have crushes on each other. There was a swimming area for kids, and horseshoe pits and barbecues under shady trees and stuff like that, and it hadn't yet gotten so hot that people shut themselves indoors all day long.

"It's good that so many people come here. Otherwise this would be a perfect spot for my dad to take me on a garbage-eating expedition," I said.

Bahar laughed.

I might explain that my father liked to take me survival camping with absolutely nothing, just to see if we could make it through a weekend living like animals and eating whatever we could find, which sometimes included bugs cooked in *somebody else's* discarded beer can. And he pretty much forced me to go with him too, just like he occasionally forced me to wear the official Scottish kilt of Clan Abernathy on his randomly proclaimed "kilt days" at the golf course. Both of these things were intended to make me tougher and more manly—to grow up—but I don't think either of us, Dad or me, got what he was hoping for out of kilts and camping.

It was the week before Blue Creek's Flag Day parade, and school had just gotten out for the summer—for good, as far as I was concerned.

Enter the dancing spiders.

Bahar said, "Your dad *does not* make you eat garbage, Sam."

I puffed up my chest like a lawyer delivering an emotional closing argument. "On the contrary, Bahar. It's actually worse than garbage. He's boiled creek water in somebody else's used beer can to make it *safe for drinking*, if it's even possible to wrap your head around that notion."

We followed the path beside the lake as it veered off between the red clay diamonds where teams of kids played pickup baseball.

Bahar shook her head and said, "Ew."

"To be honest, Dad's toasted grasshoppers on a stick weren't that bad. They kind of reminded me of an overdone corn dog at Colonel Jenkins's, but I seriously *cried* actual tears when his boiled earthworms refused to be swallowed without a slimy fight."

"Well, that's still pretty brave, if you ask me," she said.

I never in my life thought I was brave about anything.

I definitely was never brave about errant foul balls cutting through the sky like missiles while a bunch of boys screamed "Heads up!" at me, which is what happened just as I was feeling dizzy about Bahar telling me I was brave, which was also *definitely not* something that was crushy.

And the ball—a blazing line drive—would have hit me square in the face too, if it hadn't been for Bahar grabbing my shoulder and pulling me down into a crouch, without even hesitating.

That ball was hit so hard, it would have knocked my head completely off my shoulders.

The kids who'd been playing ball ran over to the three-foot-tall chain-link fence that enclosed the outfield just as Bahar and I got back to our feet. Brenden Saltarello came trotting over from home plate holding a bat in his hands, apparently the boy who'd knocked the foul ball toward us; and Brody Bjork (a kid I distinctly disliked for having participated in trapping me inside a locker and causing an extreme episode of claustrophobia) rested his glove hand on top of the fence and said, "Ha! I guess all that 'Pray for Sam'[26] stuff paid off! She pretty much saved your face from getting an extra mouth, Well Boy!"

Then all the baseball kids in the field laughed and nudged

---

[26] "Pray for Sam" had been printed on a few thousand shirts during the time when I'd been trapped in a well for three days. Some people in Blue Creek still wore them, and every time I saw one or someone said "Pray for Sam," I felt like running away and hiding.

each other, and said boy stuff about "Pray for Sam," and "The Little Boy in the Well," and other dumb[27] middle-school-going-into-high-school boy things.

So if I had been feeling any level of boost at all from Bahar telling me she thought I was brave, it was gone in an instant of dread when I realized that the two of us should never have chosen this particular path to walk home.

"Gosh, I'm really sorry about that, Sam and Bahar. Are you guys okay?" Brenden asked. He was wearing a pink Princess Snugglewarm T-Shirt that had small wet circles of sweat around his neck and under his arms. No kid in Blue Creek would ever make fun of a guy like Brenden Saltarello for wearing a Princess Snugglewarm shirt, while I couldn't *not* get made fun of by kids in Blue Creek, no matter what I wore, or said, or did.

It was all hopeless.

"I'm okay," I said. "Bahar is just like my Betsy. She would have given you a heart transplant if you knocked my face off."

And Brenden laughed, because Princess Snugglewarm fans just get things like that.

He nodded at Bahar and said, "Let's get 'em, Betsy!" which was something Princess Snugglewarm would say to her unicorn spike just before stabbing some bad guy or another in the heart.

---

[27] (excuse me)

I walked back and picked up their stupid[28] ball that had almost killed me. Brody Bjork pointed his glove up and fanned it open, a sign that he wanted me to throw it to him, but I tossed the ball to Brenden, who barehanded it and then popped it off the tip of his bat back to the pitcher's mound.

---

[28] (excuse me)

THE HUNGRY BLACK MOUTH

Everyone and everything, it seemed, had been conspiring against our finding out the truth about the Purdy House.

Two days had passed since our first Monster People meeting at the library, and Karim was still staying at my house. The three of us had tried to get together on Monday after my lunch shift at Lily Putt's, so we could read the next article Bahar had saved for us, but Mom insisted on taking me to the big mall in Uniontown so she could buy new high school clothes for me. Worst of all, Mom asked Karim and Bahar if they wanted to come along, which was incredibly embarrassing, just thinking about Bahar watching my mom pick out things for me to wear. And I knew Mom would make me try on everything and show my friends how I looked, and Bahar had very strong opinions on what kinds of clothes boys in high school should wear, despite the fact that Pine Mountain Academy had strict uniform and ties-for-boys rules. The fact that I didn't care—or even think—about my clothes made me feel kind of inadequate around Bahar too.

It was like I was going to be on display or something, modeling all those creased khaki school uniform slacks, cardigans, and stiff-collared white shirts, because Dylan and Evie were there too, contributing to the size of my clothes-shopping audience.

I knew something terrible was going to happen, but over the last year in eighth grade I'd gotten pretty good at not telling anyone when I felt doom heading my way. I was sweaty and shaking, and hardly said a word while Mom led us through the section with the big hanging sign overhead that said BACK TO SCHOOL, BOYS!

Bahar nudged my elbow and said, "Are you okay, Sam? You don't look right."

To be honest, I think I said something to her, but I can only picture my mouth opening and closing like a goldfish pressed against the side of its bowl.

Then Mom handed over an armful of stuff that smelled like the inside of a new car and told me, "Go try these on. And let us see how every one of them looks. We'll wait here."

I noticed that Bahar was looking at me, but I didn't quite understand why. I felt awful, suddenly caught up in worrying about all the things I'd never get to do here in Texas again, and then getting mad at myself because what was I thinking? I've never been clothes shopping with Bahar—not once in my life—and it was something I never wanted to do again.

Never.

Bahar held Dylan's and Evie's hands, half in an attempt to keep them from following me into the dressing room. She said, "Don't worry, Sam. It'll be okay."

So they all watched me like I was some kind of knight about to enter a cave filled with dragons, while I stood there, face-to-face with the hungry black mouth of a department store dressing room.

What I should have done was said, "Mom, maybe we could go in there together so you could check if there's a changing room with a window in it."[29]

Or I could have said, "Can Karim go in with me?"[30]

Or I could have said, "I trust the accuracy of modern clothes manufacturers. When they say size M, you can bet they are a spot-on match for a kid my size! I mean, look at me, Mom. I am the walking, talking poster child for an eleven-year-old boy who is size M!"

Which is what I did say, but then Mom shoved my shoulder playfully, nudging me in the direction of the hungry black mouth, and said, "Don't be silly, Sam! We won't have time to come back here again before we leave for Oregon."

Which is also when all the spiders in my stomach rose up in some kind of wild, flailing polka dance.

I took a deep breath and went inside the changing room.

---

[29] But that would have been weird because nobody ever wants a window in their changing room.

[30] But that would have been SUPER weird, and besides, Karim would *never* stop making fun of me if I said something like that.

ANDREW SMITH

Alone.

Well, alone not counting the ten thousand spiders.

The dressing rooms were like tiny prison cells made from windowless, floor-to-ceiling flat panels of pale-blue indoor-outdoor carpeting that seemed to suck all the sound out of the air—probably to muffle the anguished screams, I thought.

I headed left (that was the direction that said ←MEN AND BOYS) and then turned right, down a narrow hallway with three doors. The hungry black mouth vanished behind me, like I had been swallowed and was on my way to its stomach.

The clothes I had draped over my arm suddenly became unbearably heavy.

I concentrated on taking deep breaths, but it felt like there was no air in the air.

I could do this, I kept telling myself. If I couldn't, I'd end up ruining everything.

I tried the first door, but when I rattled the knob, it was locked, and a kid's voice came through the panels of indoor-outdoor carpeting.

"Stay out, you weirdo! Can't you see the door's shut? I'm putting on pants!"

"Oh. Sorry."

He was probably mad at his mom, too.

The second room was unlocked, the door halfway open.

Back when I was in grade school, my parents brought me

to a therapist to help me with my claustrophobia. My therapist was named Dr. Greene, but he always insisted I call him Matt, which made me feel weird because I didn't call any grown-ups "Matt." Kids in Texas are not allowed to call adults anything that doesn't start with an official title, like "Mr." or "Dr." or "Officer" or "Coach."

As far as I knew, no grown-ups in Texas even *had* first names.

I practically needed another therapist to help me get over calling Dr. Greene "Matt."

Matt gave me a couple of tricks to use when I started to feel my claustrophobia coming on. Matt told me I should think of something really boring, so I thought about Science Club at Dick Dowling Middle School, but it wasn't working. The clothes in my arms were getting heavier, and the dressing room—the stomach—seemed to be getting smaller. Matt also said that I could try to imagine doing something that made me very happy, so I thought about staying up after bedtime, making and eating popcorn, and watching the Cooking Channel while it rained outside. That was one of my favorite things to do.

But even that wasn't helping me.

In Mom's defense, I think it was easy for everyone in Blue Creek to just assume that Sam Abernathy—forever the Little Boy in the Well—had grown up and out of those feelings of being lost and closed off from everything. Sometimes I got lucky, and I didn't have to remind them—like when Mom and Dad decided to drive to Oregon instead of taking me to school on a plane. I could never get inside an airplane.

So I should have said something about not wanting to go into those dressing rooms that day, instead of just expecting that Mom might have known better. But to her, Dylan, Evie, Karim, and Bahar, I'm sure everything that day just seemed so perfectly back-to-school-shopping-ish, while in my mind I was trapped in the dark just like I had been when I was four years old.

It was a nightmare.

Cooking Channel, Science Club, Cooking Channel, Science Club . . .

Maybe I could just leave the door open, I thought.

And right about then, everything went black.

THE RETURN OF BARTLEBY

"Someone grew about a foot and a half since the last time I saw him!" Bartleby said.

Even though the last time Bartleby had seen me was about nine months before, near the beginning of my eighth-grade year at Dick Dowling Middle School, and there was no way I could have grown that much, I didn't bother pointing out Bartleby's obvious exaggeration.

"Where did you come from?" I asked.

"Ha! Is that any way to say hello to your best nonhuman friend, Sam?"

Bartleby tugged at the whiskers under his chin with a curled and yellowed armadillo claw. Then Bartleby's eyes shifted from side to side like a lawyer preparing to argue for an obviously guilty client's innocence. "Uh. You don't have any pets, by any chance, do you?"

Mom was allergic to cats and dogs. At least, that's what she always said.

"No," I said.

"So like I said, is that any way to say hello to your better-than-best nonhuman friend? Anyway, I dug a tunnel," Bartleby said.

"It's fifteen miles from Blue Creek to the Uniontown Mall," I said.

Bartleby pursed his armadillo lips and nodded. "Yeah. And I would have been here sooner, but I ran into a bunch of rocks and a buried Cadillac under the old graveyard. But that doesn't matter now, because you've got some important things to do, Sam!"

"Like what?" I said.

"Well, for starters, you've got to snap out of this being-afraid-of-going-to-school thing."

"I don't know. It's not the going-to-school thing that's bothering me; it's the *going* thing. I think I'm too small to leave Blue Creek. Thinking about being at school in Oregon with a bunch of kids who are all practically grown-up is really scary. I don't think I'm smart enough or good enough. I feel like I'm not ready."

Bartleby snorted a disgusted hiss. "That is *not* the Sam Abernathy I've known for . . . for . . ."

Then Bartleby clicked his armadillo claws together like he was counting.

"For . . ."

Bartleby sighed and said, "Help me out, Sam. I think I ran out of claws."

"Eight years," I said.

Bartleby's lips stretched wide in a toothy armadillo grin. Also, he had very bad breath. "Eight years! Yes, sir! The Sam I met while I was digging around eight years ago—he was no quitter! He would have left Blue Creek on the spot! And what you're about to do—going to school and learning how to be a great chef—this is exactly what *that* Sam Abernathy would have wanted more than anything else! So, kid, tell me this: Who are you, and what did you do with the *real* Sam Abernathy?"

And when Bartleby said "real Sam Abernathy," his eyes got big and dark, like he was confronting a swindler at his front door.[31]

But, as always, Bartleby was right.

I sighed.

Bartleby continued, "And another thing. No. Two more things, Sam. First—and this is very important—if you go inside that house, it would be nice if you'd look for Ishmael. Everyone misses him. Just tell him we're all down in the basement if you see him. Not the regular basement, the one that's way down below. You know, the one you've been to before."

I had no idea who Ishmael was or what Bartleby was even talking about.

"What house?" I said.

Bartleby shook his head. Little bits of dirt fell from his whiskers. "You know, Ethan Pixler's place. Well, his wife's

---

[31] If armadillos *had* front doors, that is.

house, technically. I mean, it's not her house anymore, right? Because she's dead and everything."

"The Purdy House?"

"Yeah. Whatever. The one with the secret hideout down there. And the other thing is . . . is . . ."

"Is what?"

"I forgot," Bartleby said. "Hang on. Give me a minute."

I looked at Bartleby.

Bartleby looked at me.

Lots of time passed, but I knew Bartleby was not someone I could push.

Bartleby scratched his armadillo chin.

"Dang," he said.

Bartleby had forgotten.

"It must not have been very important," I said.

"Of course it was important!" Bartleby said, obviously a little ticked-off. "Just because something's important doesn't mean you can't forget it! I mean, just look at you! Someone whose name happens to be 'Sam Abernathy' obviously forgot to put on pants, right? Isn't putting on pants kind of *important*?"

And when Bartleby said "important," he jabbed his armadillo claws in the air at my bare legs.

I looked down and noticed that Bartleby was right.

I didn't have pants on.

I felt myself turning red, and then I wondered if this was

one of those kinds of dreams where I'm at school or cooking dinner for company in my underwear.[32] I was so embarrassed. I must have been trying on my school clothes for Mom when the claustrophobia happened and Bartleby showed up.

And then I remembered where I was and what I was *supposed* to be doing, which was also about the same time that Bartleby remembered what else he wanted to tell me.

He clicked his armadillo castanet-claws together. "Now I remember what I was going to say! It's about your girlfriend—the one you have a crush on and take walks with and have iced tea with—"

"I so do *not* have a crush on her!" I protested.

"Aww. Now, Sam—" Bartleby began, in that tone of his where I could tell he was about to explain something to me that I already knew but didn't want to admit. And at the exact moment when Bartleby said "Sam," another voice came from behind me:

"Sam?"

I half jumped.

"Sam?"

It was Karim, standing in the wide-open doorway of my dressing-coffin.

Apparently, I'd neglected to shut the door too.

I turned back around, but Bartleby was nowhere to be seen.

"Sam? Why is your door wide open, and why are you stand-

[32] (excuse me)

ANDREW SMITH

ing there in your underwear? We've been waiting for twenty minutes, so your mom sent me in to see if you're okay. . . . And, Sam, WHY IS THIS EVEN HAPPENING TO ME RIGHT NOW?"

Karim, never one to miss an opportunity to overdramatize a non-event, covered his eyes and turned around.

I felt myself turning even redder (if that was possible), and getting mad at the same time too. I was mad at Bartleby for saying I had a crush on Bahar and then disappearing; I was mad at my dumb[33] claustrophobia; I was mad at Karim for walking into my dressing room[34] when I didn't have any pants on; I was mad at my mom for taking me—and everyone else— shopping in the first place; and I was mad at Blue Creek for just being so Blue Creek.

I dug around in the pile of loose clothes I'd placed (and forgotten about) on the bench inside my dressing room, and found the old Sam-shorts I'd worn for the Uniontown Mall shopping expedition, and pulled them on.

"You can turn around now, Karim," I said. "Just do one thing for me. Tell my mom that everything fits perfectly fine. I just want to get out of this—excuse me—stupid store."

Karim said, "Oh. You had that *thing* happen again, didn't you?"

I was so mad, I felt my voice shake and crack. "I don't want

---

[33] (excuse me)
[34] Even if the door was wide open.

her to know that I'm scared about leaving, Karim. Everyone's expecting me to do this, and I'm going to do it. Just don't say anything about it, okay?"

"Nobody *wouldn't* think you'd be scared about going away, Sam. Anyone would be scared to leave home."

"Would *you* be scared?" I asked.

Karim rolled his eyes and shrugged. "I'd be terrified, Sam."

Sometimes—on rare occasions—Karim could actually let his guard down and show people he truly cared about things in ways he was usually too sarcastic to be honest about. That's why everyone liked him as much as they did.

Karim helped me gather up all the school things I was supposed to be trying on for Mom.

He said, "Just leave it to me, Sam. I'll take care of everything."

BATMAN, ROBIN, AND THE GREAT DEPRESSION

"Every one of these outfits fits him perfectly, Mrs. Aber-nathy," Karim said, holding up the armful of clothes I'd sup-posedly been modeling. "Except for these blue shorts—they fit, but Sam thinks they make him look fat."

Mom gave me a hurt and concerned look that seemed to say, *Why didn't you let me see?*

Bahar stared at me. I could tell she knew that something was wrong. Maybe it was just me. Or maybe she could tell from the tone of Karim's voice that he was running his distraction play.

But Karim, always on his grown-ups game, handed the blue "fat shorts" clipped onto their plastic hanger back to my mom. He said, "The reason he was in there for so long is that he was on the phone to that Pine River school, or whatever it's called, asking about if there were specific-colored socks that are required for their uniform."

"Oh. I didn't think about that!" Mom said. "So, what did they say, Sam?"

I was lost, but Karim didn't miss a beat.

He said, "Sam told me they'll kick you out and send you home if the socks are anything other than black, fire-engine red, or white."

My mom nodded and said, "Fire-engine red! I really appreciate schools that enforce discipline!"

"Me too!" Karim said, looking at me and grinning with every tooth he had.

Fire-engine red.

So I almost died when Mom led us all into the boys' pajamas, socks, and underwear section, right in front of Bahar. Dylan kept squealing, "Underwear!" and Evie laughed and laughed. So there was ultimately nothing I could do to get through the ordeal, except immerse myself in the dread that in just a few weeks I was going to find myself about two thousand miles away from Blue Creek.

And I thought that maybe saying good-bye to all this would be more of a relief than a curse.

I was going to have to say good-bye to all this.

Nothing, no dread, embarrassment, or disappointment, could stop the spiders.

But right now, thanks to Karim, I was hopelessly lost inside a clothes-shopping nightmare, looking for fire-engine-red socks with half the kids in my neighborhood.

I was mortified.

Mom picked out some pajamas with soccer balls on them for me.

ANDREW SMITH

Karim announced to everyone that pajamas with soccer balls were probably less likely to get me beaten up than pajamas with Princess Snugglewarm on them (but I still thought Princess Snugglewarm was better than soccer). And then Mom said the worst thing a mother could say to a twelve-year-old boy in front of a fourteen-year-old girl he kind of liked[35] and who was also the cousin of his best friend, which was this: "Oh! These are so cute! Do you like these undies, Sam?"

And Mom held up a package of size ten/twelve boxer briefs with Batman and Robin on them and fanned them around in front of *everyone*, which included Bahar and my little sister.

Karim started laughing so hard, I thought we'd have to call the paramedics.

And yes, my mom shamelessly uses words like "undies" in front of my friends.

Bahar stared at me and said, "Sam. You wear *those*?"

"Not right now, he's not! Sam's are camo today!" Karim blurted out.

I felt like there was enough heat coming off my forehead to trigger a fire alarm or something, and as I waited for the store's overhead sprinklers to activate, I just said, "Fine. Whatever, Mom. Can we be done now, please?"

It was horrible.

And while Karim laughed and laughed, Mom waved her

---

[35] But who—and let me make this perfectly clear—I did NOT have a crush on.

hand and the stupid[36] package of Batman and Robin under-wear in the air at me, and said, "Stop being silly, Sam."

It was probably something worthy of an internet search—trying to see how long it would take someone like Bahar or Karim to forget about something like my *undies*, but twenty-four hours was probably not the right answer. And now here we were, the next day, all sitting on the floor in my bedroom with another article in front of us from the *Hill Country Yodeler*, while I was waiting—just waiting—for one of my friends to bring up something embarrassing about Batman and Robin.

It was bound to happen, I thought. Maybe Karim was just playing me like a hooked largemouth bass.

"Anyone who has a dead raccoon electrically wired with a lightbulb screwed into its head is statistically much more likely to participate in the occult arts than people who don't," Karim said, studying his checked-off list of the things he'd concluded about the new residents of the Purdy House.

Karim's theory sounded reasonable to me.

And Bahar said, "Maybe they named the raccoon 'Little Charlie.'"

Ever since the Monster People had moved into the Purdy House, it seemed that nobody in Blue Creek had seen or even noticed them. The only one of us who had seen them at all was Karim, on that first morning before sunrise when he'd snapped

---

[36] (excuse me)

the picture with the movers and the people watching from the porch, and the ghostly little boy standing in the upstairs window.

But you could tell that someone was living—or *residing*, I should say—in the Purdy House. Sometimes the drapes in the windows would be open, and later they'd be closed, and there was an old orange Volvo station wagon parked in the circular drive on the other side of the iron gates, which still had the NO TRESPASSING warnings posted on them.

Empty moving boxes had been piling up on the front porch.

"This next article is a feature about the Purdy House," Bahar said. She handed Karim and me each a couple of photocopied sheets of paper. "It's from 1933, during the Great Depression," she said.

And then, sure enough, Karim did it. He said, "I wonder if kids in 1933 had Batman and Robin on their *undies*. What do *you* think, Sam?"

I glared at my friend and reminded him coldly, "I cook food for you, Karim. And I enjoy mayonnaise."

The April 18, 1933, issue of the *Yodeler* was a little more modern-looking than the 1919 version. The front page had stories about President Franklin Roosevelt throwing out the first pitch of the baseball season at a game between the Senators and the Athletics; an editorial essay about whether or not Texas was going to legalize beer; a story on Winnie Ruth Judd, who chopped somebody up and traveled to California with the body parts in a suitcase; a news report on a woman from Brownsville who'd been granted a divorce from her wrestling champion husband, who "would not stay home"; and a feature on Blue Creek history—in particular, on the Purdy House.

Blue Creek History:[37]
A Look Back at the Notorious Purdy House

The town of Blue Creek has long been fascinated with the fabled Purdy House, the notorious landmark which has stood unoccupied for nearly thirty years, ever since the mysterious disappearance of its last owners, Ervin Purdy and Cecilia Pixler-Purdy.

Whether or not the house is haunted, as many of Blue Creek's townspeople contend, the history of the home and its odd inhabitants has perplexed curious citizens for decades.

Originally called the Pixler House, the stately home was constructed in 1881 by Ethan Pixler and his young bride, Cecilia, new settlers to Blue Creek.

Ethan Pixler gained notoriety and scorn as

---

[37] Apparently, at some point between 1919 and the Great Depression, people around here stopped calling it Blue Creek-Town.

ANDREW SMITH

a ruthless criminal who had robbed no fewer than a dozen banks in south and western Texas. Pixler was arrested, tried, and hanged outside Blue Creek in 1888 amid rumors of a vast, hidden, and secret fortune. None of the money stolen during Pixler's legendary robbery spree has ever been recovered.

It was a scant three months after the execution of Ethan Pixler when his widow, Cecilia, married a traveling vaudevillian, a hypnotist named Ervin Purdy who had established some reputation for his entertaining antics and miraculous feats across Texas and southern Oklahoma. Ervin Purdy claimed to be able to restore vision to the blind through hypnosis, although he had been arrested in Kansas for swindling an entire church congregation out of thousands of dollars with a fraudulent talking-armadillo scheme.

It was shortly after their marriage, in 1889, that Ervin Purdy and his bride adopted the celebrated boy known as "Little Charlie," an undersized youth reported to have been raised by wolves in the wilderness of south Texas.

Besieged by the surprising number of journalists and charitable organizations wishing to study the boy, Mr. and Mrs. Purdy began to advertise the haunting of the house by Mr. Pixler's angry spirit. Many local citizens familiar with the Purdys have said this was a means of discouraging intrusion into their lives.

The story of Little Charlie only serves to add more complexity to the rumors surrounding the house, the fates of Cecilia Pixler-Purdy and her second husband, and the mystery of the rumored hidden fortune of Ethan Pixler.

The oft-recounted story claims Little Charlie was rescued from a family of wolves by a band of outlaws who used the boy for entertainment purposes in saloons and at town fairs. The Wolf Boy was ultimately traded to immigrants from Germany in exchange for three bottles of liquor and a mule, but his new family found the boy impossible to pacify. Little Charlie, the Wolf Boy of Juno, as he'd been called, reportedly scratched at himself incessantly, chewed on household furnishings, constantly tore away his clothing, rolled his naked body on the carcasses of decaying animals, and howled inconsolably every night. He was said to only tolerate eating raw meat, and was blamed for the killing of many of the settlers' small animals, as well as those of their neighbors.

Ultimately the German immigrants became so frustrated with Little Charlie's intractability and unwillingness to learn the German language that they gave the wild boy up for adoption to Mr. and Mrs. Purdy in the summer of 1889.

It was in the years following the adoption that the story of Mr. and Mrs. Purdy, Little Charlie, and the Victorian home they lived in became a matter of increasing speculation, rumor, and fear. Townspeople in Blue Creek often reported wails and painful howls emanating from the house at night, and the youngster, Little Charlie, became a rumored suspect in the disappearance of household pets and livestock around Blue Creek. On three occasions, Little Charlie used his bare hands (which had frequently been described as claws) to dig up the casket of Ethan Pixler, prompting the Purdys to excavate a shaft and bury Pixler more than fifty feet below ground, in an attempt to get the savage child to stop exhuming Pixler's remains. Mr. and Mrs. Purdy, beleaguered by the rumors and gossip around Blue Creek, became housebound recluses, and were not seen in public for months on end.

Some witnesses reported sighting a large black figure that arose at night into the air above the roof of the house, and unsubstantiated claims of human bones and open graves on the inner grounds have fed into the unfavorable reputation of the home.

The house itself became a site of scorn, and residents of Blue Creek eventually avoided passing anywhere near it throughout the 1890s. Ervin Purdy and Cecilia Pixler-Purdy entirely ceased interacting with neighbors. There were frequent reports of strange lights and noises from within the Purdy House, and shadowy figures watching like demonic sentinels from the home's upper, darkened windows.

In 1905, the Purdy House was locked and shuttered behind its imposing iron gates. Mr. and Mrs. Purdy, and their adopted son, Little Charlie, had disappeared entirely from Blue Creek some months earlier, never to resurface anywhere up to the time of this story's publication.

The house has remained sealed, fueling speculation, primarily among Blue Creek's young folk, about a sinister haunting presence that has never been substantially verified.

"So, basically, both these articles only give everyone *more* to be afraid of about the new people and the Purdy House,"

Karim said. "As soon as the poison gas dissipates and they come back from the nudist colony in Mexico, I'm going to ask my parents to move."

"You already did move, Karim," I said, pointing to the camp cot my dad had put in my bedroom for him. "And if you want to, you can just use my phone and call your mom and dad, who are probably enjoying a quiet evening together, alone, at your house, which is about a two-minute walk from here."

And then I added, "I can't get over the fact that ten pounds of potatoes cost twenty-one cents in 1933."

There were food ads at the bottom of the page.

"In my opinion, both of our articles only show how exaggerated and overblown the story is, how prejudiced people around here can be, and that there is nothing really dark or sinister about the Purdy House at all," Bahar said, continuing to be, as always, so *Bahar*.

And really, everything Bahar said made perfect sense to that grown-up part of my brain, even if the regular part of my brain was willing to throw all reason overboard and side with Karim as far as his policy of staying the heck[38] away from the Purdy House forever.

---

[38] (excuse me)

WHAT EVERYONE NEEDS TO KNOW ABOUT THE MONSTER PEOPLE (PART 3)

What Everyone Needs to Know about the Monster People:

✔ Have not been seen in daylight. May be vampires.

✔ Have a lamp made out of a dead raccoon.

✔ Have a hideous black flying beast that is bulletproof and comes out of their house at night during all the screaming.

✔ Have a coffin buried fifty feet below the ground to keep the Wolf Boy from digging it up again.

AN EMPTY PAIR OF SHOES AND
THE DESTRUCTION OF PARIS

Anyone in Blue Creek who'd ever posted a résumé on the bulletin board of Trey Hoskins's Teen Zone in the public library had to know that it was NOT the most popular place for prospective employers to conduct recruitment searches, unless they wanted someone like Michael Dolgoff to wrangle up a can of hellgrammites,[39] or to possibly get some yardwork and babysitting or something, but nothing that required any real talent or skill.

I mean, I should know because I'd never been called for any home chef services by anyone who'd been to the library, and my "Help Offered" flyer had been posted in the Teen Zone for almost six months. When I'd put it up, Karim had told me that it wasn't a good selling point to list that I was well versed in the preparation of gooseneck barnacles,[40] since the people of Blue

---

[39] Hellgrammites are really disgusting bug larvae that bite, but people like using them for fishing bait, because apparently fish will eat anything that fits into their mouths. Hellgrammites most closely resemble the worst things you could ever see in a nightmare.

[40] I'll admit it, they look horrible, but not terrifying like hellgrammites.

Creek were more than satisfied with the chicken-fried steak on a stick at Colonel Jenkins's Diner. I was beginning to think Karim was probably right about the barnacles. And I realized I probably made things worse by also listing that I knew how to make gnocchi, which, like gooseneck barnacles, nobody in Blue Creek had ever heard of.

However, I had been hired two times from an ad I'd hung at Lily Putt's—once to make a thirtieth anniversary dinner of beef Wellington (that's so 1980s!) for Mr. and Mrs. Rubenacker, who owned the movie theater, and another time to prepare merit-badge cookies for Blue Creek Boy Scout Troop 116.

Blue Creek's most successful teen entrepreneurs always seemed to be the boys who mowed lawns in spring and summer, or those who climbed up on roofs in foul weather to clean out rain gutters in fall and winter. Gnocchi in brown butter sage sauce or gooseneck barnacles in lemon cannot compete with free-flowing rain gutters in Blue Creek, I suppose, no matter what the weather's like.

"One time, Brenden Saltarello found an entire dead squirrel when he was scooping out the rain gutters on Mrs. Benavidez's house," Karim told me. "The squirrel's head came off in Brenden's hands when he picked it up."

"Does he still clean gutters?" I asked.

"Yes, but he's a vegetarian now," Karim said.

That explained why all those times I'd seen Brenden playing golf at Lily Putt's with some of the other guys on the baseball team, he'd never ordered a burger from me at the snack bar.

And ever since she'd turned fourteen, Bahar had picked up a few jobs babysitting around Blue Creek, all from the flyer she'd posted in the Teen Zone. Still, I had to conclude the following:

Gooseneck Barnacles > Unclogging Disgusting Rain Gutters with Dead Squirrels in Them > Babysitting

Because it was just after we read the 1933 feature on Blue Creek history and Bahar had talked (actually, "argued" is a more accurate term) me and Karim into walking back to the library with her so she could photocopy the next article she'd found about the Purdy House, when her parents texted Bahar to tell her that she needed to come home right away because there was a young family of prospective clients that was interested in employing her to babysit their offspring.

So Karim and I were free and off the hook.

Or at least that's what we thought, as Bahar once again joined the ranks of the employed.

"Maybe you guys can stay here and read it on your own," Bahar said. "In 1962 it was like one of those old sci-fi movies here in Blue Creek, what with the Cold War going on, and a screwworm infestation and all."

"Screwworm infestation?" I asked.

"It was a tense time," Bahar said. "I don't know where people got their ideas from all those years ago."

"Everyone smoked cigarettes then, even on TV shows," Karim said. "The chemicals they put in cigarettes can make you go insane."

I nodded in agreement. On the other hand, my dad and I had eaten a lot of trash and bugs on our survival campouts, and eating garbage was probably just as bad for your sanity, but I didn't want to confess that to Karim and Bahar.

So after Bahar left us there in the library, Karim and I took advantage of our freedom and sat down on one of the big red couches in the Teen Zone, slipped our shoes off, put our feet up on one of the ottoman cubes, forgot all about screwworms and what Bahar wanted us to read, and watched everyone who'd come in for Tuesday Teen Gamer Afternoons. There was a tournament going on, and everyone was playing this game called *Battle Quest: Take No Prisoners*, which was totally confusing to me, but there was a lot of shooting and things blowing up in it, so it probably had to be better for you than cigarettes or eating garbage.

There is something that becomes unavoidable in the lives of Princess Snugglewarm fans. In the same way that I'd been hypnotically drawn to Trey Hoskins's wall display for A. C. Messer and *Princess Snugglewarm versus the Charm School Dropouts* when we'd walked into the library on Sunday, my eyes latched on to a familiar shade of pink T-shirt, and a magical unicorn who had a blood-spattered horn named Betsy, which was worn by one of the boys sitting at the consoles where everyone was waging war on everybody else.

Princess Snugglewarm fans are all okay people, as far as I'm concerned.

I bumped my knee into Karim's so I could get his attention.

"Hey. Brenden Saltarello's over there playing in the *Battle Quest* tournament," I said.

Karim shifted uncomfortably beside me on the couch. He said, "I'm going to go somewhere quieter so I can read that article Bahar gave us."

That was something I did *not* think Karim would voluntarily do.

And I'd just been getting comfortable. On the big projector screen, some gamer had blown up the Eiffel Tower. Several of the kids there were mad about it and were dropping giant cucumbers from dirigibles; some high-fived each other. I couldn't tell which side of the war Brenden was on—if he liked France or not.

I said, "You *are?*"

"Yeah. The 1962 one, right?" There was a little bit of urgency in Karim's voice, but judging by his jittery legs, I figured he had to go to the bathroom or something.

"Um."

And then Karim was gone. He left me there alone on the couch, watching the violence and destruction of Paris from enormous bomb-laden cucumbers on the main screen in the Teen Zone, with only his empty shoes to keep me company.

I waited there on the couch for Karim to come back, but

after an hour had gone by and the entire planet had been pretty much destroyed by teenage video gamers and exploding vegetables, the tournament finally settled with a noisy victory from a high school boy, and the Teen Zone quickly began emptying out.

Trey Hoskins, whose hair was magenta that day, found me sitting there alone and asked why I hadn't been playing in the tournament. I told him the truth—that whatever side I was on would have gotten mad at me because of how horrible I am at video games, especially ones that use vegetables for evil as opposed to good—and then he reminded me about returning the new Princess Snugglewarm graphic novel by Saturday morning, and coming in to see the author, A. C. Messer. I assured him that I would, that I had already finished reading *Charm School Dropouts*, and it was the best one ever, so I'd probably read it a few more times before I had to bring it back. Trey knuckle-bumped me in approval, and then caught me staring at his hand when he did.

Trey Hoskins's fingers were totally purple.

He said, "That's what happens when you do this to your hair and you don't have gloves."

Then Brenden Saltarello walked toward us. In my entire life, I'd probably said fewer than a dozen words to Brenden Saltarello, outside of the usual "Hey" or "Thank you for not knocking my face off with your baseball," and stuff like that. And inevitably, the "Hey" routine would happen again. But I could see why Karim liked him. Everyone liked Brenden Saltarello.

When Brenden passed by, he said, "Thanks for the game, Trey."

And Trey said, "See you Saturday, Brenden."

Of course Brenden Saltarello had to be planning on coming in Saturday to see A. C. Messer talk about Princess Snugglewarm. Nobody who wore a shirt like his would *ever* miss the opportunity to meet the actual creator of the Princess Snugglewarm universe. Just thinking about it made me excited, like it was my birthday coming up or something.

Then Brenden did a chin nod at me and said, "Hey, Sam."

I did a chin nod back. "Hey, Brenden. That's a great shirt."

"Oh. Thanks." Brenden Saltarello looked down at the carpeted space between the ottoman and sofa, and said, "Why do you have so many shoes?"

I didn't know what to say. This was a question I had not been expecting. So I said, "Oh! You never know when you might need more shoes."

Brenden Saltarello just looked at me for a few seconds of awkward silence, like he was thinking I was probably the stupidest kid in the world, which is totally what I felt like. Then he shrugged, glanced back at my "extra shoes" one more time, and left.

Karim did not come back.

I looked down every aisle, in every possible research area,

but he was gone, and I was a little bit mad about being abandoned at the library by my best friend.

So I texted him.

SAM: Hey. Where are you???

KARIM: Pike Street. Almost at your house.

SAM: Why?

KARIM: Because you said I could stay over.

SAM: No. Why did you leave?

KARIM: …

SAM: Karim?

KARIM: I wanted to read the article Bahar told us about. It was too noisy in TZ.

SAM: You are walking all the way to my house in your socks.

KARIM: Not really. They're your socks. I borrowed them when you were at LP yesterday.

SAM: …

KARIM: Sam?

SAM: …

KARIM: Sam?

SAM: I put your shoes in the lost and found.

KARIM: 😂

SAM: …

KARIM: My mom's going to be mad at you.

SAM: When the poison gas goes away and she gets

back from the (excuse me) nudist colony in Mexico with your dad.

KARIM: 😂

SAM: …

KARIM: Did you really leave my shoes in lost and found?

SAM: No. I am carrying them like a dummy. I'm almost on Pike.

KARIM: Thank you. Sorry for ditching you.

SAM: Why did you leave? Never mind. You don't have to tell me.

KARIM: Yeah. BS.

SAM: Karim! EXCUSE YOU.

KARIM: No. I meant Brenden Saltarello.

SAM: Oh. Oops.

KARIM: 😂

KARIM: I'm at your house now.

SAM: I'll be there in like ten minutes.

KARIM: Your mom asked me where my shoes are.

SAM: Well? What did you think she would do?

KARIM: I told her that you won them from me in a poker game behind the liquor store with some old men who just got let out of jail.

SAM: …

KARIM: Sam?

SAM: …

KARIM: Sam?

SAM: . . .

KARIM: Well, she is pretty mad at you for gambling, and she told me she was going to make you give me my shoes back. She's getting me some ice cream right now, btw.

HAUNTED HOUSES, LABORATORIES, AND WINDMILLS

"No one better be gambling in there, or both you guys are going to be in a lot of trouble," Dad said through my closed bedroom door.

Dad seriously could have taken a few lessons from some of the teachers at Dick Dowling Middle School on how to make authentic scary-sounding threats to twelve-year-old boys.

What was Dad thinking? I don't even know how to play poker.

"We're not gambling, Dad. We're reading. I promise."

I glared at Karim, the magic lie-telling machine, who just grinned and shrugged.

It turned out that Bahar had been right about screwworms—whatever those are.

The front page of the *Hill Country Yodeler* had several stories. One was about the opening of the Austin County Fair; another was about how the county had run out of money for its screwworm eradication program;[41] another

---

[41] I read the whole article, hoping to learn what screwworms are, but the story didn't say, so I suppose everyone in Texas knew what screwworms were in 1962, and so maybe I'm glad that we don't have a screwworm crisis today.

was about how Boy Scout Troop 116 needed to find some new recruits because they were down to just five boys who were all brothers and one cousin; and one was the story Karim and I had been tasked with reading, which was an article about how the town of Blue Creek was attempting to sell off the Purdy House in order to raise money to purchase a new fire truck.

Blue Creek's Plan to Sell off Unwanted House to Purchase New Fire Truck Goes Bust

Blue Creek's Town Council is looking for a spare $37,651.48 in order to purchase a much needed fire truck, and they just might have found a solution to their problem: auctioning off the long-abandoned Purdy House. The scheme may have paid off, if only it weren't for the ghosts and all the other things that go bump in the night.

Last week's "Fishing for Fire Trucks Fund-raiser" at the annual Blue Creek Days celebration only managed to raise a woeful $348.52 toward the targeted cost for a new pumper truck, $38 thousand.

"Three hundred and fifty dollars won't buy much more than a few dozen buckets and some sand shovels," said Blue Creek's honor-

ANDREW SMITH

ary mayor, Brock Skoog, who is also the varsity baseball coach and civics teacher at Blue Creek High. Skoog added, "You can't put out a Russian-atomic-bomb-generated house fire with buckets and shovels."

Skoog said, "We're going to need top-of-the-line emergency equipment, given the dangerous actions of the Soviets in our hemisphere, and the Purdy House has sat vacant long enough. The people of Blue Creek should put the home to good use in order to benefit everyone. Winning this crisis means preparedness."

It is not the first time Blue Creek's Town Council has attempted to sell the Purdy House. The house was put up for auction in 1933, but at that time there were so many foreclosures in the county that the property attracted no bids whatsoever.

Skoog had been hoping for a better outcome with this attempt, since the home has now stood unoccupied for more than half a century.

Unfortunately for Blue Creek's all-volunteer fire department, after Skoog and a group of citizens spent a troubling night in the mysterious Purdy House, hopes for making the sale—and purchasing the new fire truck—have all but vanished like the mists of a nightmare.

"After what I saw there, you won't ever get me to step foot anywhere near that house, not ever again," said Blue Creek Realtor and hair salon owner Annabelle Hoitink.

Mrs. Hoitink and a group of other council members including Skoog, Patrick Snipes—honorary mayor from 1958—and Shirley Beverly, wife of Cal Beverly of the Blue Creek Fire Department, all spent Tuesday evening inside the old estate in an effort to dispel persistent rumors about the haunting of the Purdy House.

The evening may have been a bust for the Town Council, however, as no more than forty-five minutes into the experiment, all the guests fled the house in fear.

"Almost as soon as we got inside the home, there were odd noises like muffled screams, doors opening and closing by themselves, objects moving in front of our eyes, and two of the guests claim to have seen a shadowy image of a boy standing alone at the top of the staircase," said Mrs. Hoitink.

"No one in their right mind would ever spend five minutes in that wretched place," Hoitink exclaimed.

ANDREW SMITH

At this point, the Town Council has decided to yet again postpone the auction of the house, with no date determined as yet for when another may be held.

"Who would ever want to buy that place?" asked former mayor Patrick Snipes, adding, "And as far as the new fire truck is concerned, all of Blue Creek might be better off burning down if it will serve to get rid of that particular abomination."

"And those were reasonable people—*responsible grown-ups*—who couldn't even last one hour alone in the Purdy House," Karim said.

I nodded and glanced at my window, which was pointing in the direction of Karim's house, which meant it was also pointing at the Purdy House beyond.

"No wonder it's been empty for so long," I said.

The new people—the Monster People, as Karim preferred to call them—had been in the house since Sunday, but nobody had seen them, and the town of Blue Creek hadn't burned to the ground yet.

When Dad knocked on my door to call us out for dinner, we both jumped.

Karim took a deep breath and said, "I've had enough of this Purdy House stuff. I wish those people never moved here."

And just as we were catching our breaths and about to join the rest of my family in the kitchen, both of our phones buzzed with a message from Bahar:

You guys! The people I'm babysitting for are THE PEOPLE who moved into the Purdy House.

Karim looked like he was about to throw up.

I texted back:

Wait—Did you tell them YES?

And Bahar replied:

It was too late to do anything about it by the time they brought me here. They have a little boy. Named Boris.

Bahar was texting us *from* the Purdy House.

There was so much swirling around in my head at that moment. Bahar's words "it was too late" were almost as troubling as the fact that the little boy was named Boris, which sounded like the name of every villain in every scary movie ever made.

"They're probably going to turn Bahar into their thrall now," Karim said.

I didn't know what a *thrall* was.

"What's a thrall?" I asked.

"You know how in horror movies, a lot of times monsters have humans who are brainwashed into doing whatever the monsters want? Like luring victims to haunted houses and laboratories and windmills and things? That's what a thrall does."

Karim knew a lot about monsters and stuff.

My dad knocked on the door again and said, "Guys! Come on before your corn dogs get cold!"

And Bahar sent another text:

I'm about to go inside now. You guys should come over here.

WHAT EVERYONE NEEDS TO KNOW ABOUT THE MONSTER PEOPLE (PART 4)

What Everyone Needs to Know about the Monster People:

✔ Have not been seen in daylight. May be vampires.

✔ Have a lamp made out of a dead raccoon.

✔ Have a hideous black flying beast that is bulletproof and comes out of their house at night during all the screaming.

✔ Have a coffin buried fifty feet below the ground to keep the Wolf Boy from digging it up again.

✔ Have a kid named Boris.

✔ May be transforming Bahar into a mindless thrall with no will of her own.

THE LOSER OF THE WAR OF JENKINS'S EAR

No one who had lived in Blue Creek for the past century had ever summoned the guts to go inside the Purdy House, maybe with the apparent exception of four people who only lasted three quarters of an hour there.

And now Bahar—my best friend's cousin, someone who was nice to me when she didn't have to be, someone who I kind of "liked"[42]—was for all we knew hopelessly trapped inside the most haunted house in Blue Creek, and possibly all of Texas, for that matter.

Knowing this, how were Karim and I *ever* supposed to concentrate on an intellectually uninteresting dinner of corn dogs and potato puffs?[43]

To make matters worse, my little brother, Dylan, who was almost four years old, had somehow gotten it into his uncivilized

---

[42] Let me be clear: not in the same way that Karim fell so easily into his very serious type of "like" that made me nervous to even think about because it involved such things as holding hands in public and voluntarily kissing people who are not your parents, like Hayley Garcia or Brenden Saltarello.

[43] This meal was NOT my idea.

head that mayonnaise was the same thing as whipped cream, and was going through what Mom called a "phase" where he put mayonnaise[44] on everything, which included potato puffs and corn dogs. So all this ended up making Karim nervous, scared, sad, nostalgic, and heartbroken.

And that's a lot of powerful competitors playing tug-of-war with the neuron ropes inside the head of a twelve-year-old boy. Besides, how nostalgic could anyone who's only lived twelve years actually be?

Throughout dinner, Karim kept his head down in order to avoid making eye contact with Dylan's bottle of mayonnaise.

It was probably too soon, I thought.

"Is something the matter, Karim?" Mom asked.

So, of course Karim answered with a spontaneous practicing-to-be-a-teenager lie. "No, Mrs. Abernathy. I'm fine. It's just Tuesdays are my usual days for doing yoga, and since I skipped it today on account of reading and studying all day with Sam, I figured I'd do some during dinner. This is the Loser of the War of Jenkins's Ear[45] pose."

And then Karim sunk his chin a bit lower, inhaled deeply, and added, "It's reformist yoga."

Dad perked up like a pressure cooker full of popping corn.

"Hey! I wonder if Kenny or James Jenkins are related to the ear?"

---

[44] From a squeeze bottle, unfortunately.
[45] This was an actual war, fought in the 1700s over someone's actual severed ear.

ANDREW SMITH

"No, Dad," I said. "No."

Karim stayed with his head down. If he kept this up, I figured he was probably about to start chanting or something in about ten seconds.

And Dad continued, "Everyone does yoga these days. Maybe after dinner you could show me some slick moves, Karim!"

I didn't know *where* my dad got his ideas from. Half the time I questioned whether it was even possible that we were related.

I pointed out, "You can't do yoga in a kilt, Dad. Not even *reformist* yoga."

My father liked wearing the official kilt of Clan Abernathy.

"Heh-heh. I guess you're right, Sam," he said. Then Dad put his chin down just like Karim did, assuming the Loser of the War of Jenkins's Ear pose from *reformist yoga*, and asked, "What am I supposed to feel?"

Embarrassment, I wanted to say.

"Besides, Karim and I promised we'd go visit Bahar after dinner. She's babysitting, and we didn't want her to be alone. She gets scared sometimes," I said.

Karim suddenly broke out of his Loser of the War of Jenkins's Ear pose. His head shot up and he stared at me with an expression that in reformist yoga would probably be called a You're Crazy If You Think You'll Ever Get Me Inside a Haunted House pose.

IF IT MAKES YOU FEEL GOOD, BELIEVE IT

"**Someone has obviously *not* been paying attention to all** the homework we've been doing," Karim said. "Are you out of your mind? Do you really think I'm going to go over to *that* house? Have you been brainwashed by Communists or something?"

"I have two words for you, Karim: 'Jenkins's Ear,'" I said.

Karim nodded like a scientist receiving a Nobel Prize. "That was some of my best work."

I don't know where he got all his ridiculous stories from.

The sun was down. Karim and I were cutting through the clearing in the woods by my house, past the pile of concrete and construction rubble that had been used to seal off the dangerous and abandoned "Sam's Well," which had become a kind of local landmark in this part of Texas.[46]

"I'll walk there with you, but I will *not* go inside," Karim said. "In fact, I may just stand outside my own house and watch

---

[46] Our second-most favorite local landmark was the giant T. rex hazard at Lily Putt's Indoor-Outdoor Miniature Golf Complex.

or take pictures when you get swallowed up by the black beast that rises from the rooftop."

I was doing my best to coax him into a walk to the Purdy House.

And Karim was not the most encouraging friend to have along when you're going on the scariest mission you've ever been on.

But worse than Karim's stubbornness and the fact that there was no moon this evening and it was getting dark quickly, was the fact that Bahar had not answered the last text I'd sent her (which I'd sent three times). And that text said this:

SAM: Is everything okay?

BAHAR: . . .

SAM: Is everything okay?

BAHAR: . . .

SAM: Bahar?

BAHAR: . . .

SAM: Is everything okay?

"Maybe her battery's dead," I said.

"If it makes you feel good, believe it," Karim said.

"Maybe it's on silent and she put her phone down somewhere so she could tuck Little Boris into bed."

"Did you say 'Little Charlie'?"

"No. Stop it. 'Boris.' Duh."

"If it makes you feel good, believe it," he repeated.

"Maybe there's a solar flare and it's causing spotty coverage at the house," I said.

"If it makes you feel good, believe it."

"You're not being very helpful, *Karim*."

"Throughout history, that's what people have always said to realists, *Sam*."

"A realist wouldn't be afraid of going to the Purdy House. And a realist wouldn't believe the exaggerated claims made by people in the *Hill Country Yodeler*. Because realists only ever think about things that are . . . uh . . . *real*."

"If it makes you feel good, believe it."

"Is that like a chant from your *reformist yoga* or something? Because it is definitely not making me *feel good*," I said.

Then Karim said, "Hang on a second. Stand still. I want to capture the Sam Doing the Dumbest Thing He's Ever Done in His Life reformist yoga pose."

"Ha. Ha. Very funny." I kept walking. Karim was about three steps behind me.

I said, "Maybe she dropped it and it broke."

"If it makes you feel good, believe it."

This could have easily gone on long enough for me and Karim to walk to Oklahoma, but we were coming up on the dirt road behind his place, and the roof of the Purdy House was already in sight, peeking through the gaps in the treetops.

And when we walked through the side of his yard, Karim

said, "I'm going to go inside for a second and check in with my parents, and maybe get some more clothes."

"You're really going to leave me out here to go there alone?"

"What would my parents think if I didn't come in?" Karim asked.

"They'd probably think it's nice vacationing together in Mexico," I said.

"Ha ha. Whatever, Sam. See you in a few. Maybe. If you make it back."

And without even turning around, Karim trotted off and disappeared inside his front door.

So that was that, and I was stuck wanting to run back home and lock myself in, while desperately wondering what was going on with Bahar inside the Purdy House.

And I thought, *Where is Princess Snugglewarm when you really need her?*

LITTLE CHARLIE HEARS MY CALL

One does not simply disregard the NO TRESPASSING signs that hang on the gates of the Purdy House.

I mean, in many ways the notices themselves looked more menacing than the two-word warning emblazoned across each of them. The signs had to have been a hundred years old, white, with peeling oxidized red uppercase letters painted on metal that oozed streaks of rust like blood, and here and there bubbling scabs where corrosion had been steadily decaying upward through their surfaces.

If the signs came to life, they would truly be monsters.

I had never been this close to the Purdy House in my entire life. Now here I was standing just inches from the gates. I did not touch them, however.

The lights were on in every window, except for the ones on the third floor and in the attic. Naturally, haunted houses never have lights on up there. The old orange Volvo was gone, and the porch stood, silent and cluttered with empty boxes.

I tried a text again:

Hey, Bahar, I'm outside the gates right now.

Then I thought to play off all the ridiculous things that I'd been imagining (or not), like it was just another Tuesday night in Blue Creek:

How's it going with the babysitting? ☺

And:

How's the dead raccoon? ☺

Followed by:

What kind of food do they keep in their refrigerator? ☺

You can always tell so much about people by the food they keep inside their refrigerator, just like you can tell a lot about people by the dead animals they use as lighting fixtures.

I waited. Crickets and cicadas seemed to be yelling at me from the dark. I imagined an entire insect kingdom arguing about whether or not the little kid they were watching should knock—or try to actually *open* the gates to the Purdy House. I looked up into the sky above the roofline of the house. No gigantic black-winged beast blotting out the stars. Then I got mad at myself for even thinking about a gigantic black-winged beast, because Bahar would have told me how irrational I was being.

But the thing was, Bahar was not telling me anything.

There was still no answer from her to any of the text messages I'd sent.

I reached up and made a fist, cocked it back like I was *intending* to knock. But if I knocked on the gate, nobody inside would hear it, and it would probably hurt my knuckles on top of everything else. So I formed an *O* around my mouth with my hands, aimed myself between a gap in the iron bars of the gate, and whisper-shouted, "Bahar!"

To be honest, I've been louder in libraries and nobody ever gave me a second look.

I tried it again. "Bahar?"

But I still couldn't get much volume. My throat was just too tight.

So I braced myself for what I knew I had to do: I decided I would simply open the gates, step up to the front door of the Purdy House, and knock like someone inside owed me money or something; like I had a job to do.

Easy, right?

I lowered my hand to the latch.

"HEY! WHAT ARE YOU DOING?" Karim shouted at me from across the gravel road in front of the Purdy House.

And I screamed louder than I had ever screamed in my life.

Then Karim screamed louder than he had ever screamed in his life.

And for just a fraction of a second, as Karim and I were both screaming and I was turning away from those old creepy gates to run for my life, I thought, *This must be why they called it the Screaming House.*

I caught a glimpse of Karim standing along the roadway as I darted from the gates. His eyes looked like headlights on a fire truck, and he was pointing a hand up toward the house behind me.

"He's up there!" Karim shrieked.

I glanced back, and sure enough, up on the third floor[47] one of the narrow windows had been illuminated, and standing there, perfectly still and ghostlike, looking down to precisely where Karim and I were experiencing sheer terror, was the figure of a pale little boy dressed in what looked like one of those old nightshirt things that people used to wear a century ago.

"It's Little Charlie the cannibal!" Karim said.

I was so scared that there were literally tears leaking from my eyes.

And I thought, *Me. I am the kind of food they keep in their refrigerator.*

Karim was right behind me, which kind of made me feel like I was being chased, so I ran faster. And then everything got much, much worse when Karim began to yell, "There's something crawling on me! There's something crawling on me!"

Which made me run even faster, which made Karim run faster too.

We did not stop running until we had gotten back to the clearing near Sam's Well. Then Karim and I both collapsed into the grass of the field, where we panted and gasped for several minutes before we finally calmed down enough to say anything.

What was crawling on Karim was a cicada as big as my

---

[47] Did I mention that attics in haunted houses are places where no lights are ever *supposed* to be turned on?

hand. It had gotten inside his T-shirt, and Karim had the creature balled up in a twisted wad of shirt.

"Sam. Can you get this thing off me?"

I do not touch cicadas. Not ever. Karim knew that.

In fact, I am as afraid of cicadas as I am of any imaginary demons and ghouls that may or may not haunt the Purdy House. I can't even look at a cicada without wanting to give up on life entirely.

"Karim, you're my best friend, but no."

And the trapped cicada inside Karim's T-shirt made a soft and terrifying little hideous scream, which is what trapped cicadas do sometimes.

"Some friend you are," said Karim, who'd been living in my room since last Sunday.

He got to his feet, and keeping the wadded-up cicada tangled inside his hand, he pulled his T-shirt off and threw it on top of the mountain of concrete and rebar plugging the opening to Sam's Well.

And I said, "You were the one who left me to go to the Purdy House all alone."

"You didn't quite get there, did you?"

"You screamed at me. That's why," I said.

"I wouldn't have screamed if I hadn't seen Little Charlie getting ready to eat you. I saved your life," Karim said.

"If it makes you feel good, believe it," I said.

I stood up and shook out my clothes, just in case any other

cicadas had decided to hitch a ride away from the Purdy House.

"You owe me a shirt," Karim, who had already ruined a pair of my socks today, told me.

I just shook my head. Panting, exhausted, and terrified, we started back toward my house. I couldn't really tell if we were mad at each other, but I'm pretty sure we were. Best friends get that way sometimes.

"So. Who's going to be the one to do it?" Karim asked between gulps of air.

"Do what?" I said.

"Go tell Bahar's mom and dad that Bahar is now a powerless thrall for the Monster People," Karim answered.

"Well. It's *your* aunt and uncle," I said.

"But *this* is all your fault, Sam," Karim argued. "You have to do it."

As was so often the case, I couldn't follow Karim's logic that any of this[48] was my fault.

"For all we know, Bahar's probably got a lightbulb coming out of her head," Karim said.

"She should have told them no as soon as she saw it was the Purdy House."

And then Karim, always the devoted cousin, said, "Did you make anything for dessert? I'm kind of hungry again."

---

[48] And by "this" I meant all the stuff that Karim and I had convinced ourselves was happening, while having no concrete proof to back up our wild assumptions.

CANNIBALS DON'T EAT NOODLES

No one told Bahar's parents that their daughter had been transformed into a mindless thrall for the Monster People, because in the end, Karim and I decided that a "wait and see" approach would be the wisest strategy for us to pursue.

Anyway, we had no choice since we couldn't agree on whose job it was to break the news to them. We argued about it for the rest of the walk home, but fell silent and grumpy through dessert.

It was chocolate-banana crepes, which I did make, by the way.

I was so mad at Karim for not being brave enough to go to Bahar's house and warn her parents that I didn't even tell him about the chocolate sauce he had on his face. I let him go to bed like that. And then he woke up that way too, stained with a dark brown slash across his cheek.

At breakfast, Dylan and Evie laughed at him.

And Mom, who would happily adopt any straggler that Dad or I brought into our home, just shook her head sadly and grabbed a damp dishcloth. And as she gently wiped the chocolate sauce[49] from his face, she made big love-eyes at Karim and said, "Oh! You poor sweet thing! I bet you miss your mom!"

Then she combed his hair with her fingers, which kind of made me mad because hand-combing of a boy's hair is something that I *believed* Mom was only allowed to do to Dylan, or possibly to me, but only if there were no other middle-school-aged boys around to witness it happening.

Karim shrugged and said, "Well. I'm not really missing Mom and Dad, Mrs. Abernathy. Um. They came home yesterday from the nudist retreat in Mexico, but Mom and Dad were so sunburned, they asked me if I could stay away from home for a little bit longer. They can't really move, and they look like the flag of Denmark."[50]

Mom said, "Oh, sweetie! You can stay here as long as you'd like."

It was a good thing breakfast was oatmeal, for two reasons: (1) I was near to choking from listening to Karim's wild fabrications, and (2) Mom was acting like she was about one step away from actually chewing Karim's food for him.

Luckily for all of us, Karim's phone began buzzing inside his Teen Titans pajama pants pocket.

"That must be Denmark texting you," I said.

---

[49] The sauce was made with Valrhona Équatoriale, which is known as perhaps the world's finest chocolate for sauce-making.
[50] Which is red.

Karim pulled out his phone and looked at the screen, then at me.

"It's from Bahar," he said.

"Oh my gosh! Is she okay?" I asked.

Then Mom got this super-concerned mom-bird look on her face.

"Did something happen to *Bahar*?" she asked.

"Um." I glanced at Karim, but his perpetual-motion lie generator hadn't kicked into first gear yet. Even he didn't know what to say to Mom.

But Mom's concern could only be sustained for a moment, because Dylan had climbed down from his booster seat and was foraging in the refrigerator for some mayonnaise, which he fully intended to put on top of his oatmeal.

I nudged Karim. "He's probably possessed by the same mayonnaise demon as Brenden Saltarello," I said.

So we got up from the table and went back to my room while Mom and Dylan got busily involved in a heated, endless-loop-with-a-three-year-old argument about whether or not mayonnaise was an acceptable topping for oatmeal.

Then Dylan started to cry.

And Evie started to cry too, because nobody was paying attention to her.

"Is it like this every morning?" Karim asked me.

I shut the door behind us. "Only for about the past year now," I said. "What did she say?"

"Didn't you hear her? She said, why did Dylan always get his way, and she wanted bacon on her oatmeal," Karim answered.

"Not Evie. *Bahar*."

"Oh."

Karim dug his phone out and opened the group message Bahar had sent us. I turned mine on too. Normally I would feel a little dumb[51] for group-texting with Karim if he was in the same room as me, but since I was kind of mad at him, and since he was wearing one of *my* T-shirts and what was most likely another pair of *my* socks, I decided that dumb[52] was not exactly what I was feeling.

> **BAHAR:** I'm sorry I didn't text back last night. Boris hid my phone and said he wouldn't tell me where it was unless I entertained him properly all night, and only when he was tired enough to go to sleep, which wasn't until after midnight.
>
> **BAHAR:** Boris says cell phones are bad for you, and that they eat away your identity, and he could tell that my identity was almost entirely eaten already. He said he would probably like me more after my identity was completely erased, because he knew he didn't like me as soon as he saw me. He's really creepy.

---

[51] (excuse me)
[52] (excuse me)

SAM: Like scary creepy?

BAHAR: Idk. Like weird. He made me feel bad. He kept telling me he didn't like me very much, and that he wouldn't mind if I hid in the closet for the rest of the night, because he wouldn't try to find me if I did, and that he was certain I'd probably never be happy in life.

SAM: Wow. How old is he?

BAHAR: 6

SAM: So did you entertain him?

BAHAR: I tried telling him stories, but he said he didn't like stories as much as he'd like me to be quiet. They had some books there, and I tried reading him one, but he said he didn't like books as much as he'd like me to go to sleep and have a nightmare. Then we colored for a while.

SAM: Did he like coloring?

BAHAR: No. He told me I was a fake babysitter and that I was probably stuffed with noodles, and if I fell down and cracked my head open on their very steep and creepy staircase, he would eat them. So I thought maybe he was hungry, and I asked him if he wanted a snack, but he told me he doesn't like snacks as much as he likes babysitters who never talk to him, and then he wanted to take a bath, but his mother always puts an entire gallon of milk in the bathtub for him.

ANDREW SMITH

KARIM: See? He wanted to eat Bahar. He's Little Charlie the cannibal.

BAHAR: Cannibals don't eat noodles.

SAM: Did you put milk in the bathtub?

BAHAR: They didn't have any, so I poured in two cans of Diet Coke.

SAM: You let a kid you were babysitting take a bath in Coke?

BAHAR: Diet Coke.

BAHAR: I didn't know what else to do, he made me feel so useless. I just wanted him to stop not liking everything I tried to do.

KARIM: Did Boris turn you into a thrall?

BAHAR: No. Don't be dumb.

KARIM: But you let him take a bath in Diet Coke. How can we be sure?

BAHAR: Trust me. You CAN be sure. You're dumb, K.

SAM: What was the house like?

BAHAR: Really, really weird. Lots of very creepy taxidermy everywhere.

KARIM: How's the raccoon?

BAHAR: One of its legs is completely bald. Its fur is falling off.

SAM: We were outside last night by the gates, but we got scared and left.

KARIM: We saw Little Charlie up in the window, that's why.

SAM: Karim got a cicada in his shirt, that's why.

KARIM: It was screaming.

SAM: Does Boris wear those old nightshirt pajamas like ppl used to wear about a hundred years ago? Bc that's what we saw in the third floor window.

BAHAR: That was Boris. His parents say he's "fussy" about things. But idk. He's just weird and he doesn't like anything and he's not pleasant at all.

KARIM: Nobody says words like "pleasant" anymore.

KARIM: That's the kind of word a thrall would use.

BAHAR: Whatever. Meet me at the library. I found another article about the Purdy House you guys have to see.

KARIM: I'm going to be Boris and say that I don't like reading articles about the Purdy House as much as I like having screaming cicadas trapped in my shirt.

SAM: I'm cooking lunch at Lily Putt's today, and Karim will probably be here at my house while I'm gone, stealing all of my clothes.

BAHAR: Come after lunch then. You need to see what I found, Sam.

SAM: Why do I need to?

BAHAR: I found an article about your dad. And the Purdy House.

IN WHICH I COME FACE-TO-FACE (THROUGH A WINDOW) WITH BORIS

Anyone who's a stranger and just settles down in Blue Creek can generally count on being assaulted by waves of curious, casserole-bearing snoops, but not so much for the Monster People and their unpleasant child, Boris.

For the past century, with a few notable exceptions, nobody in Blue Creek ever set foot anywhere near the Purdy House. I mean, there was the drunk guy and the deputy about a hundred years ago, and then that group of anti-Communist civic leaders who wanted to sell the house for a new fire truck to put out nuclear bomb attacks, but other than that, the Purdy House was looked at as something like a toxic radioactive wasteland by generations of Blue Creekers.

A toxic, *haunted* radioactive wasteland.

And, speaking of *haunted*, all this thinking about the Purdy House inspired me to come up with a Little Charlie's Haunted Burger for Lily Putt's snack bar that day. It was made with a cornmeal-fried catfish filet on an herbed buttermilk biscuit bun, topped with ghost pepper sauce and sweet orange, fennel, and cilantro relish.

It might have been too daring for Blue Creek, but most things usually were.

So it was just about an hour before my lunch shift was supposed to end, and I was mentally preparing myself to head over to the library and meet up with Bahar and Karim, when I saw the little unpleasant kid who had stopped by for no reason at all the other day, outside of his mission to tell me how much he didn't like anything I tried to do.

Which is precisely when it dawned on me: that crusty-nosed kid, the same one who'd told me how much he didn't like *thigh chicken*, had to be the same Boris who Bahar had babysat the night before.

Unpleasant Boris had come back to Lily Putt's Indoor-Outdoor Miniature Golf Complex, undoubtedly for no other purpose than to simply spread joy and make people feel good about themselves.

I was so excited by my realization that I wanted to run to the library just so I could tell Bahar that I knew who Boris was too, and that I could confirm how very unpleasant he could be. But Dad would get mad at me if I ducked out early and left a mess in the snack bar, so I decided to do the next best thing, which was to take a picture of Boris with my cell phone and text it triumphantly to Bahar and Karim, kind of like a trophy shot for a big game hunter.

　　　　　　　　　　　　　　　　　　　　ANDREW SMITH

Unfortunately, while I was snapping pictures of him through the window of the order counter, Boris looked directly at me. I was busted.

There are few things more obvious and unsettling to someone than when a stranger is taking pictures of them with a cell phone.

Boris put down his putter and golf ball, and headed straight toward me and the snack bar, marching determinedly across the hole-four putting fairway.[53]

"Why did you take a picture of me?" he asked through the little opening in the order window.

And at that moment, I tried to think of all the possible explanatory lies that Karim might come up with on the spot, but my mind was as erased as any thrall's in the controlling grasp of his vampire overlords.

Where was Karim when I needed him?

Probably in my room taking a nap, or going on a shopping spree for clean clothes in my dresser, I thought.

"I. Uh. I thought you were someone else," I said.

I decided I really needed to get some pointers from Karim. I was such an awful liar, and avoiding the truth was something that might come in handy for me when I started high school in what amounted to just a matter of days.

The baby spiders in my stomach began to stampede.

---

[53] Hole four had a six-foot-tall Ferris wheel on it, and you had to get your ball to go inside one of the passenger gondolas so it could be dropped off on the other side.

"Who?" the little kid asked.

And I already didn't even know *who* he was talking about.

"What?"

"Who did you think I was?" the kid asked.

And being the unpracticed liar that I was, I suddenly couldn't think of the name of a single other living human being. So I said, "Uh. Um. That kid who was in the War of Jenkins's Ear."

And the little unpleasant boy on the other side of the order window just stared at me without saying a word.

So I figured that (1) if this actually *was* Boris, that made him six years old, in which case there would be no way he had ever learned anything about the War of Jenkins's Ear, which started in 1739, unless he really was a vampire and was actually *in* the War of Jenkins's Ear, but (2) it was daytime and sunny out, so he couldn't be an eternally undead vampire since he wouldn't be able to tolerate sunlight, at least not according to everything I'd heard about vampires, and (3) if he was only six years old (and simultaneously Boris), he wouldn't be here at Lily Putt's all alone, which meant (4) his really creepy and mysterious parents were probably somewhere nearby.

He kept staring. His mouth was closed, and there was no expression at all on his face. He could have been asleep, if it weren't for his unmoving, never-blinking eyes.

"But I was obviously wrong," I said. "Would you like something to eat today?"

I smiled.

The kid stared.

"What do you have?" he asked.

And here we go, I thought.

"Today at Lily Putt's Indoor-Outdoor Miniature Golf Complex, our chef has prepared a special Little Charlie's Haunted Burger."

There was no way I was going to tell him what was on it.

"Who's Little Charlie?"

There was also no way I was going to tell him that Little Charlie was a wild boy who'd been raised by wolves and was probably also a cannibal, and that he used to live in the same *haunted house* this extremely unpleasant customer on the other side of the window currently lived in.

So I just stared at him, taking a page from his playbook, saying nothing.

But this boy was top-notch at staring in silence.

Then he cracked. He said, "Your name is Sam Abernathy, isn't it?"

I nearly toppled from the milk crate I was standing on. But then I thought, Nobody *doesn't know* who Sam Abernathy is, since just over seven years ago the Little Boy in the Well put Blue Creek on the map. I could imagine a Realtor sitting down with Boris and the Monster People and skirting the whole LEGEND OF THE PURDY HOUSE thing by explaining to them, *You've probably already heard about the little boy named*

Sam Abernathy who was trapped in a well for three days here in
Blue Creek! Well, you'll be delighted to know that the famous well
is now a kind of local landmark, and it's just a few hundred yards
away from your beautiful front porch!

Yeah, that had to be it.

I squinted like a sheriff in an old Western.

Boris squinted back, like the fastest draw in Texas.

"How do you know my name?" I asked.

"Your girlfriend is my babysitter," the unpleasant little gun-slinger said.

And that was exactly when I lost my footing on the milk crate I was standing on, and I tumbled down onto the cold tile floor of Lily Putt's snack bar. While I was down there, out of Boris' sight, all I could think was, Where did he get the idea that I was Bahar's *boyfriend?* What did Bahar *say* about me? Why would she even mention my name to him? Was he only guessing, just to make me feel uncomfortable?

That had to be it, I decided.

I straightened my apron, righted the milk crate, and climbed back up to the counter. My knees were skinned. Boris had climbed his little self up onto the handrail for the order line, and he had raised his face high enough against the window to where he could see behind the counter.

"I thought you died just now," Boris said. "But I decided I didn't care enough about you to call nine-one-one or anything. Are you wearing a dress? You skinned your knees."

It was kilt day at Lily Putt's.

"It's a kilt. It's traditional in Scotland. And I am *not* her boyfriend," I said, then added with a pinch of salt, *"Boris."*

"Well, with how much she talks about you, anyone would think you were her boyfriend," he said. "All she does is talk. Just like you. I thought you were going to make me some food, but all you've done so far is talk."

I cleared my throat.

Boris stared at me.

I said, "What would you like?"

Then something absurd and unexpected happened. Boris said, "I'll order three of those Charlie burgers."

It still felt as though we were facing off in the middle of a dusty street in the old Wild West. "Very good. You must be hungry."

"Do they come with fries?"

I knew what he was getting ready to do, and I wasn't falling for it this time.

I said, "You'll find out in about five minutes."

Then I spun around and went to work.

PART THREE
ON BECOMING A THRALL

IN WHICH I COME FACE-TO-FACE (THROUGH A WINDOW) WITH THE MONSTER PEOPLE

Everyone has at one time or another done something impulsively, without really thinking things through ahead of time, and then walked away from the wreckage of that decision wondering, *Did I really just do that?* Or, *Is this all some kind of weird trance?*

Right?

And that's pretty much exactly what I was asking myself as I took what felt like a sleepwalker's journey (in a kilt) from Lily Putt's to the Blue Creek Public Library to meet up with Bahar and Karim.

Did I really just do that?

Because here's what happened: After I bagged up unpleasant Boris's order of three Little Charlie's Haunted Burgers,[54] I began cleaning the kitchen in order to leave for the day.

But just as I was about to leave, there came a familiar rapping of dirty little knuckles against the glass of the snack bar's order window.

---

[54] I served them with mini polenta hush puppies and *not* fries, which I was sure Boris would have told me ahead of time that he did not like.

Tap tap tap tap tap!

"Hey. Hey. Kid. Hey. You. Bahar's boyfriend. Are you still in there? Hey."

I stood behind one of the prep tables, where Boris couldn't see me.

"I told you I am *not* her boyfriend, and I was off work at two. Rigo, my coworker, will be here to help you in just a minute, if you don't mind waiting."

I stood there for a moment, silently considering the possibility of ducking out the back door as quietly as I could. Unfortunately, there wasn't an actual *back* back door in the snack bar. It was more of a side door facing the seventh hole, and Boris would certainly see me if I tried to leave. You'd think the guy who designed a mechanical llama hazard might have had the good judgment to install an escape hatch in the snack bar. One of these days, when Lily Putt's was mine, I'd make that addition, I thought.

More knocking.

"Hey. Kid. Hey. I don't want anything. My mom and dad just want to ask you something. Are you there? Did you fall down again? Hey. Hey."

Wait.

Mom and dad?

The monster child had monster parents, and they wanted to talk to *me*?

I tried to compose myself.

I could see by the shadow on the window that Boris had climbed up onto the handrail and was trying to look down at the floor to see if I had fallen down and died again.

"There is no climbing allowed here at Lily Putt's Indoor-Outdoor Miniature Golf Complex," I said as assertively as any twelve-year-old kid in a kilt could.

Boris knocked again. "I said my mom and dad want to ASK YOU SOMETHING."

Dad would be mad at me if I ignored customers, but Dad didn't have to contend with the Monster People who had moved into the Purdy House. So I took a deep breath and stepped out from behind the prep table, and this was the first of many times that afternoon when I found myself thinking, *What the (excuse me) heck am I doing?*

There they were. The Monster People, and Boris, balancing on the handrail while smearing something sticky onto my window. At first I was surprised that Boris's parents—the same people who'd showed up as grainy dark images in Karim's photograph—were not dressed in black funeral-director outfits, but the normal clothes may have been part of their ruse to fit in among the folks who lived in Blue Creek. The dad wore an Atlanta Falcons T-shirt,[55] and the mom was dressed like a receptionist at a hair salon or something.

Perfect disguises, I thought.

The dad, who had a beard but no mustache and long hair

---

[55] It was the same shirt as Boris's, only with fewer food stains on it.

that had been knotted back in a ponytail, said, "Are you the young man who cooked these fish sandwiches?"

He smiled, and I tried to avoid looking at his eyes, just because of the whole *thrall* thing that Karim had nearly convinced me of, and usually whenever someone calls me "young man," something unpleasant is about to happen.

Also, they were NOT *fish sandwiches*.

"The Little Charlie's Haunted Burgers with polenta hush puppies?" I asked, in a corrective kind of way.

Boris's mom and dad nodded, as though they had one mind between them.

"Yes," I said. "I am the chef who prepared them."

Chefs say "prepare." People who eat stuff like chicken-fried-steak-on-a-stick at Colonel Jenkins's Diner say "cook."

"Well, I just wanted you to know we *loved them*," Boris's dad said.

"Thank you."

Dad would be mad at me if I wasn't always polite, even to people who terrified me.

"You must be Sam," said the mom, in a jewel-studded jeans jacket on a too-hot-of-a-day to wear one. "Bahar told us all about you!"

Again I found myself wondering why Bahar would ever talk about me to anyone. We were *not* boyfriend and girlfriend, and I definitely *did not* have a crush on her, especially since I didn't even know what having a crush on anyone felt like. It was all so confusing. I decided I'd need to talk to James about it, even if he did tease me too much at times.

I said, "Oh."

And Boris's dad went on, "We're new to Blue Creek. We're hoping to make this our permanent home and open up a business here. We're the Blanks. I'm Timmy, and this is Beth, and I'm pretty sure you and Boris have already met each other!"

"Um. Welcome to Blue Creek," I said.

No grown-up men are ever named Timmy, I thought, especially not in Texas. The name had to be fake.

"You're also the little boy who got trapped in a well, right?" Beth Blank said.

Apparently, I was correct in my assumption that their Realtor had told them everything about what made Blue Creek famous—except for the part about the Purdy House, that is.

I squinted at Boris. He squinted back like he was waiting to see who'd make the first move. And I wondered what kind of business they were planning on opening here in Blue Creek. We already had one cemetery and one funeral home, and that was enough. And I also couldn't help but wonder about their last name: Blank.

"He's not very nice. He took a picture of me because he said he thought I was someone from a war," Boris said.

"Oh, Boris!" Beth Blank said.

"And he's not funny, either," Boris went on. "All he does is talk. And I didn't like my haunted burger. What was that stuff on it?"

"You mean orange and fennel?" I said, immediately hating

myself for falling into the black hole of Boris's unpleasantness.

"Yeah. That stuff. Orange and fennel. I never eat stuff like that because I hate it," Boris said.

And Timmy Blank, Boris's dad, said, "Boris is funny."

Hilarious, I thought.

Timmy Blank continued, "Well, Beth and I were just talking, and we'd really like to try out your catering service, so we wanted to see if you'd be available to make dinner for the three of us, plus a guest."

And this was one of those things—an impulse—that I absolutely could not control, because it involved cooking.

I immediately said, "When?"

"How about Friday night, if you're not already booked? Beth and I are going to be looking at some commercial property for our taxidermy shop, and we thought it would be fun if we ordered dinner in for all of us."

Taxidermy. Mr. and Mrs. Blank stuffed dead animals. This explained so much.

"'All of us'?" I said.

Timmy Blank cleared his throat. "Yeah. Well, we're going to be leaving to look at some more storefronts. So it would be for the three of us, and Boris's babysitter, Bahar. You're friends with Bahar, right?"

And when Timmy Blank said "friends," he winked at me.

No.

But I still couldn't help myself.

"What time?" I asked.

"Let's say six," Beth Blank said.

I had mindlessly crossed over the line and had become a cooking thrall. Or a *preparing* thrall.

"Is there anything in particular you'd like me to prepare? I have a sample menu here somewhere," I said.

Timmy Blank answered, "You can surprise us! Maybe if it works out, we'll hire you for a fancy dinner party when we're all settled in, and invite all our new neighbors!"

He obviously had no idea that none of his fancy new neighbors would ever set foot in the Purdy House.

Then Mr. Blank added, "Would forty dollars per person be fair? One hundred sixty for the dinner? And dessert, too, naturally."

"Naturally," I said. It was like I was in a trance. A hundred and sixty dollars could buy a few decent kitchen gadgets, and some Princess Snugglewarm merch.

And Boris added, "Nothing with oranges and fennels. I hate that stuff."

So, just like that, I was stuck. And all the way downtown to the library, I kept asking myself, *How did I let this happen?* The Purdy House had lured in Bahar, and that was bad enough, but now it was about to get me, too.

And there was nothing I could do about it.

I'd have to concoct some scheme to sign Karim on as my assistant, I thought.

SOMEONE'S GOT A CRUSH ON SOMEONE

"Someone who happens to be six years old and also hap-pens to be named Boris came to Lily Putt's twice in the last three days," I said. "Here. I even took a picture of him."

We were all sitting on the sofa in the library's media center. I held my phone out so Bahar and Karim could see the shot I'd taken through the snack bar's window that day.

Bahar nodded knowingly. "Yep. That's Boris."

"Taking pictures of strange little six-year-old kids is kind of creepy, Sam," Karim said.

I put away my phone. "'Creepy' doesn't even begin to describe Boris."

I lowered my voice to the kind of whisper you'd use in one of those scenes where all the lights go out in a horror film. "I saw his mom and dad, too. I talked to them. I made them all Little Charlie's Haunted Burgers. They eat *real food*. Well. I think they do, at least. I didn't actually see any of them eat anything. They only *said* they liked it."

"My theory is that Boris and his parents just absorb nutrients though their skin in the bathwater, which explains the milk and Diet Coke thing," Karim said. Then I saw him typing on his phone another entry on the list of things he knew about the Monster People.

I kept my voice in a whisper. "Yeah. But they're hiring me to cook dinner for them tomorrow night."

"Dude. You're going *inside* the Purdy House? To *feed them?*" Karim asked, horrified.

"I know. I don't know what came over me, but when they asked if I could do it, and then told me how much they were willing to pay, I just couldn't say no."

Karim shook his head and made a kind of pitying click with his tongue.

"I'll be there. I'm sitting for Boris again," Bahar said.

"Karim, you have to be my helper. Come with me," I said.

"Sorry. I don't cook, Sam."

"Please?"

"No."

"I'd do it for you," I said.

"No you wouldn't, because I wouldn't say yes to going inside that place. Not ever. What were you thinking?"

I put my face in my hands and rested my elbows on my knees. I was so confused. Maybe they *had* put me under some kind of trance-inducing spell or something.

"I don't know what I was thinking," I said.

I was on the verge of tears, but no kid in a kilt wants to cry inside a public library. Maybe I'd ask Mom or Dad to call the Monster People and cancel the catering job.

But I could never cancel a cooking opportunity. So I just sat there and tried not to cry, unsure of what I'd gotten myself into, or what I was going to do about it.

"Hey, Karim, Bahar. Hey, Sam."

None of us had even noticed that Brenden Saltarello had been there the whole time, watching a stream from a baseball game on one of the library's computers.

Karim didn't say anything.

Bahar said, "Hi, Brenden."

"I like the kilt, Sam. Pretty daring," Brenden said. "Maybe one day it'll catch on here in Blue Creek."

Then I wasn't only miserable. I was also embarrassed. I should have changed into regular Texas-kid clothes before leaving the golf course, but I'd been too disoriented and confused by what had happened with Boris and his parents.

"Huh. Maybe," I said.

I tucked my kilt between my knees and crossed my legs. I suddenly felt as though the entire world was looking at me, and it made me very uncomfortable. That was the thing about Dad's kilt-wearing requirements: sometimes I entirely forgot that we were living in Texas, which was a very big state with an unsurprisingly small number of guys who wore kilts.

"Well, I mean, I'd wear one, I think, even though my family's Italian. So there's probably a dress-code regulation about that somewhere," Brenden said.

"You could just call it a plaid mini-toga or something," I offered.

Then Brenden Saltarello laughed.

I noticed that Karim was definitely *not* laughing. In fact, he was staring with the same squinty gunslinger eyes that Boris had used on me an hour earlier.

It almost seemed that Karim was jealous or something.

I just didn't get any of this.

Brenden put on his headphones and turned back to the game he'd been watching.

Karim continued to glare.

Bahar looked at Karim, then at me, and shrugged. Then she mouthed: *Someone's got a crush on someone.*

Ugh. This was all too much for me. I could feel the surface temperature of my skin rise by about ten degrees, and could only imagine I was redder than the deepest red on my Clan Abernathy tartan. And I couldn't stop myself from wondering if Bahar had been thinking about having our usual iced tea again on Saturday, which was just a couple of days from now.

If we made it past Friday, that is.

"Uh. I really need to go home and put on some regular clothes and get some reading done for school," I said.

It felt like the spiders were doing the wave around and around and around in my stomach.

Bahar said, "Wait. We have one last article. This is the best one, Sam. You'll see why. It's from 1994, and there's someone you know in it."

I didn't want to know anyone who'd ever had anything to do with the Purdy House, but now I was stuck, and what had I been thinking? What was I possibly going to prepare for dinner for the Monster People?

WHAT EVERYONE NEEDS TO KNOW ABOUT THE MONSTER PEOPLE (PART 5)

What Everyone Needs to Know about the Monster People:

✔ Have not been seen in daylight. May be vampires.

✔ Have a lamp made out of a dead raccoon.

✔ Have a hideous black flying beast that is bulletproof and comes out of their house at night during all the screaming.

✔ Have a coffin buried fifty feet below the ground to keep the Wolf Boy from digging it up again.

✔ Have a kid named Boris.

✔ May be transforming Bahar into a mindless thrall with no will of her own.

✔ Boris absorbs nutrients through his skin in his bathwater.

✔ They have now begun an indoctrination spell on Sam.

✔ ~~SAM IS NOT ALLOWED TO TELL JOKES TO BRENDEN SALTARELLO EVER AGAIN!!!~~

✔ Their last name is BLANK.

THE OTHER ABERNATHY

No one who's twelve years old ever thinks about how their dad was also at one time a kid.

It was a truth that was too big to wrap my head around.

For all my life, my dad had always seemed so grown-up, never changing—the kilt-wearing, survival-camping, golf-course-owning, unofficial pep rally leader, ex-banker, and perennial optimist of Blue Creek, Texas.

But when confronted by the overwhelming evidence, I had to face the fact that my father indeed had once been a child, and not only that, but a child who'd apparently liked grunge rock and had at one time been arrested for breaking the law in the very town where I'd been born and spent my entire life.

"My dad must have been really relieved the day I fell into the well," I said. "That way, for sure all the people in Blue Creek would stop talking about *him* and only talk about the *other* Abernathy."

Because this is what the 1994 article from the *Hill Country Yodeler* revealed about my dad and the Purdy House:

Blue Creek Teens Detained after Being Trapped inside Abandoned Purdy House

Three incoming ninth-grade students from Blue Creek High School were arrested Friday night after finding themselves trapped inside an empty house on North Detweiler Road.

The teens, Davey[56] Abernathy, 13, Oscar Padilla, 14, and Linda Swineshead, 13, all recent graduates of Dick Dowling Middle School, unknowingly locked themselves inside the long-abandoned Purdy House after accepting a dare from incoming members of the Blue Creek High School freshman football squad, to spend three hours inside the shuttered home on the night of last week's full moon.

"We sure didn't mean to cause any problems," Abernathy said. "We just wanted to show we were brave enough to do it, because the other boys had been making fun of me and Oscar. Linda didn't want us to go there, but she came along so she could stop us from doing anything stupid, which didn't really work out. Because once we got inside, the doors and windows seemed to lock all by themselves, and we were stuck."

---

[56] Davey? *Davey?* This was already too much to handle.

"Davey was going to do it alone, but I wouldn't let him," Padilla said. "He's my best friend, and I was afraid he'd get eaten by that cannibal ghost or something."

The Purdy House has long been rumored to be haunted, and has been the focus of several recent paranormal studies. To date, stories of a cannibalistic wild boy named Charlie Purdy, the house's fabled inhabitant, have never been substantiated.

Abernathy, wearing baggy jeans and a hole-pocked Nirvana T-shirt, was released early Saturday morning into the custody of his grandmother, gospel singer Lily Abernathy, owner of Blue Creek's Lily Putt's Indoor-Outdoor Miniature Golf Course. The sheriff has not yet determined whether charges will officially be filed against Abernathy and the other teens.

"This is a tough call. The house has sat there empty for so long, it's like nobody cares about it beyond its reputation as some sort of local nuisance. All empty houses do is attract trouble, I'll tell you. But if being dumb was a crime, there's no doubt these three kids would be facing the judge," Sheriff Cole Glick said.

Padilla and Abernathy had both recently

dropped out of the Blue Creek High summer football training session, and claimed they had something to prove to the other boys on the team who'd teased Abernathy and dared the boys that they were not brave enough to spend time inside the house, which holds a frightening reputation in Blue Creek history. The third teen, Linda Swineshead, went along in support of her boyfriend, Davey Abernathy.[57]

The three youths climbed over the locked gates and entered the house through a loose basement hopper window, which, once inside, proved to be too high for the teens to use as an exit. While the teens were inside the house, members of the Blue Creek High School freshman football team waited outside, timing the duration of the stay.

"As soon as we got inside the house, weird things started happening. We heard noises—like singing—coming from somewhere underground, and sounds like something was being dragged back and forth across the floor up in the attic," Abernathy said.

"We didn't realize that the window was

---

[57] Wait. Dad had a girlfriend when he was THIRTEEN? Named *Linda Swineshead*? I can't even . . .

too high for us to climb back out, and then Oscar [Padilla] found this little secret tunnel, but he got trapped behind the doorway, and that's when me and Linda [Swineshead] got really scared. We tried to get out of the house through the front doors, but they were sealed shut, so we went back down to the basement and started yelling for help below the window where we came in, but it was stuck shut too, and I don't think anyone heard us," Abernathy said.

After three hours had passed with no sign of Abernathy, Padilla, and Swineshead, the football players outside went to a nearby house and called Sheriff Glick. None of the players remained present at the scene to provide an account of the trespassing to law enforcement.

Speaking on conditions of anonymity, one of the football players said, "We argued about going over to tell Miss Lily Abernathy that Davey was killed, but we decided she'd find out eventually anyway."

According to Abernathy, Padilla had become trapped inside a narrow crawl space leading from the basement to a small room that had been dug deeper underground than the basement. "There wasn't any light anywhere,"

ANDREW SMITH

Abernathy said, "but Oscar told us how the place lit up by itself when he got inside, and then he started screaming at us because he couldn't get out through the little door, and he thought he saw a ghost and what looked like a coffin just sitting there in the middle of the floor, and there was an armadillo that came running toward Oscar, which really scared him because Oscar is afraid of armadillos."

Glick released Padilla and Swineshead to their parents' custody late Friday evening, while Abernathy, the confessed ringleader of the break-in, remained in the sheriff's detention until his parents could be located the next morning.

"Everyone does foolish things when they're kids," Glick said, "but breaking into that old Purdy House has got to be one of the dumbest things I've ever heard of in all my years of law enforcement here in Blue Creek. I hope those three learned their lesson and are done with it now."

When we finished reading the article, Bahar and Karim just stared at me, obviously waiting for me to confess to something that I had no idea I was guilty of.

"My dad never told me anything about getting trapped inside the Purdy House," I said.

"Maybe he's got a huge criminal record besides just that," said Karim, always encouraging. Then he added, "Being called a *ringleader* when you're only thirteen says a lot about your reputation as a scofflaw."

And Bahar said, "I wonder what he's going to say when you tell him you're going there tomorrow night."

I put my head in my hands again and said, "Ugh."

And where had Karim ever learned a word like "scofflaw"?[58]

---

[58] A "scofflaw" is a delinquent.

ANDREW SMITH

SOMETIMES CODE BETWEEN FRIENDS CAN FAIL MISERABLY

Someone was trying to call me.

We'd said good-bye to Bahar at the clearing in the woods where all the piled-up debris formed a little Texas Eiffel Tower above Sam's Well, and were heading back to my house when my phone started buzzing in my pocket.

It was James Jenkins.

And for more than just a moment, I felt conflicted about what to do. I really wanted to talk to James about so many things, but I really *did not* want to talk to James while Karim was listening to all those things I needed to ask him about.

I watched the screen on my phone, frozen for an instant on the tightrope stretched between wanting to answer it and wanting to hang up.

"Well? Aren't you going to answer it?" Karim said.

"Um."

I was stuck. I touched the connect button, but I kept walking through the woods toward my house, hoping that Karim might be distracted by the sounds of insects and my footsteps, which I tried to make as loud as possible.

"Hi, James," I said.

"What took you so long? Are you working at Lily Putt's?"

"No. I'm walking to my house, with Karim."

I said "Karim" especially loud, in a code-between-friends kind of way, hoping that James would know this wasn't the best time to talk about certain things like crushes and flirting, or being attracted to someone. And then I said, "What's up?"

James sounded so happy and relieved. "Well, I didn't think I'd make it to the end, but camp is finally finished. Everyone's leaving tomorrow, and I'll be back in Blue Creek at your house on Saturday afternoon sometime. It's still okay for me to stay over for a few days, right? My mom wanted me to make sure before she drives all the way out there. You know, it's kind of awkward for her because of my dad and football and all."

My room was sure going to be crowded for the next few days.

"Yeah. It's totally okay."

I missed James, and just the thought that we'd get to spend the last few days of summer together lifted my spirits, despite the fact that my dad was a criminal and some kind of *ringleader*—and one who had a *girlfriend* named Linda Swineshead when he was only thirteen, and I still had to come to terms with it all.

"Well, I just wanted to tell you thanks for talking me out of quitting the dance program when I wanted to. Sam, it really was the hardest thing I've ever done in my life, and I hated it most of the time because of all the work and the pain and stuff, and not having any friends here, not having any freedom, and never getting a chance to relax and just do nothing," James said.

"Oh. Well, I knew deep down you didn't really want to quit, James. You're not like that."

"And something cool happened. A group of agents came to the school and watched our final today. One of them is going to call my mom and ask her if he can send me on auditions in New York and Los Angeles. Looks like maybe we're both saying bye-bye to Blue Creek and going far away from Texas, huh?"

Cue the spiders.

"That's great news, James. I bet you're excited about that," I said.

"Well, to be honest, all I want to do for the next week is sit around doing nothing but play video games and watch movies and eat all the food that dancers aren't supposed to eat."

"I think I could help with most of that," I said, and James laughed.

"Dude. You can if you're not too busy hanging out with your crush," James said, and I could hear the tease in his voice.

I nearly choked, and Karim was practically close enough to hear what James was saying. Or maybe everything just seemed so incredibly loud at that exact moment. I decided my only chance to get out of the situation would be to intensify the encryption level of friend-code-speak and try to hang up as soon as possible.

"Heh-heh," I said. "That reminds me of that TIME we were

in Miss Van Gelder's Spanish class and those two girls who sat up front were TALKING ABOUT YOU when we came in, but they DIDN'T KNOW YOU WERE THERE LISTEN-ING, and they were SAYING STUFF that was, like, totally EMBARRASSING."[59]

"Huh? I don't remember that. What are you talking about?"[60]

"I know! You should have seen HOW RED YOUR FACE WAS, because you were RIGHT THERE ALL THE TIME. Ha ha! That was SO AWKWARD. If only they KNEW THEY SHOULDN'T HAVE BEEN TALKING RIGHT THEN."

There was a little pause, and then James asked, "Sam, are you okay? Why are you screaming at me?"

It was a struggle. But I noticed that Karim was paying more attention to me than to where we were going.

"Yeah, me too, James," I said. "We're just about to go inside. I'll call you back IN A LITTLE WHILE."

I hung up, and Karim asked, "Why were you yelling at James Jenkins like that?"

And finally tapping into a skill that I thought was exclusive to Karim, I said, "He's in Massachusetts, and they're having a really bad nor'easter right now."

"In *summer*?"

---

[59] That's friend-code-speak, if you get it. Unfortunately, it doesn't always work.
[60] See? I told you.

Karim, who had already impressed me once that day with his use of the word "scofflaw," apparently also knew more about New England weather than I gave him credit for.

But I was on my A-game.

"Climate change. It's a terrible thing."

Karim nodded solemnly.

SON OF A SCOFFLAW

"No one actually still *remembers that*, do they?" Dad asked.

Dad had come in to tell us good night. He was under the impression that Karim and I had been reading my summer assignments, which, of course, we had not been doing. And Karim instantly waylaid him with the kind of ambush question a seasoned detective would use on a guilty crime boss, which was this: "Mr. Abernathy, will you please tell us the story about the time you got arrested for breaking into the Purdy House?"

Which was when Dad expressed his shock that anyone in Blue Creek still talked about the crime spree in which he was ringleader to Oscar Padilla and Linda Swineshead, whoever that was.[61]

And I said, "No one *has* to remember it, Dad. Once something gets printed in the newspapers, it pretty much never goes away."

---

[61] I suppose I'd been feeling a little bit jealous on behalf of Mom. What would she think about Dad having a girlfriend named *Linda Swineshead* when he was just thirteen?

"Oh. Um." Dad seemed to be at a loss for words, which is a place Dad rarely found himself. "Well, it was a long time ago, boys. I was about your age, in fact, and it was just one of those nutty kid-prank kind of things that boys your age—our age—do without carefully thinking them through."

"Mr. Abernathy?" Karim asked.

And Dad didn't say anything; he just gave Karim a look like he was bracing for Karim to do what we all expected him to do.

Which is exactly what happened, because Karim added, "*I've* never been arrested, and neither has Sam—at least not as far as I know."

I was horrified. And Karim just looked at me like he was waiting for some kind of confirmation that the Sam-apple did not fall very close to the Dad-tree.

"I haven't." I shook my head.

"So what's it like? Being arrested, I mean," Karim said. Then he sat up on his narrow camp cot and put his feet on the floor, which was when I noticed that he was once again wearing a pair of *my socks*. "But first, what we'd really like to know is, What happened to you once you were all alone *inside the Purdy House*? How terrifying was *that*?"

In another era, Karim could have easily been one of those old-time radio announcers on a mystery-horror show.

Dad cleared his throat, glanced over his shoulder, and eased my bedroom door (which was open, as usual) quietly shut. It seemed almost as though he was about to reveal to us some horrible secret that needed to stay trapped inside my room, and I wasn't certain I wanted to hear it.

That closed-in and trapped feeling started coming over me.

Dad stepped over the spare mattress Mom had already put on the floor for James. Then he sat down on my bed, next to my feet. His expression was exactly like the look you'd see on the face of any kid who was getting ready to go in and get interrogated by the principal.

He took a deep breath and rested a hand on my shin. "I suppose I should have told you about it a long time ago, Sam. But I figured it didn't matter anymore, and besides, your mother doesn't know anything about it."

I wondered how full Dad's file cabinet of secrets could possibly be.

Dad lowered his voice. "It was a dare—kind of. But when I was in eighth grade, I had a best friend named Oscar, and like the other kids in Blue Creek, we used to hear all the wild legends about the Purdy House. Oscar liked to add his own ideas to the stories, and it was like the things he made up almost took on a life of their own. But Oscar and I actually wanted to *see* what was inside the Purdy House, because we knew most of the things people believed about the house were just pure fiction. Most of them."

And I thought, *Most of them?*

Dad continued, "The summer after we got out of Dick Dowling, Oscar and I decided to try out for the Blue Creek

High freshman football team. You know, back in those days every boy in town went out for football when he got into high school. It was what was expected of you. But it took us a while before we could honestly admit to each other that being on the football team over summer vacation was just not fun, not even close to being fun, so we quit, which led to the other boys on the team teasing us and calling us cowards and—ahem—worse things than that. And I don't know whose idea it was—it could have been Oscar's, but he always said it was Kenny Jenkins's—for us to prove we were tough by staying inside the Purdy House, alone, from nine to midnight one night while Kenny and the other boys on the football team waited outside to make sure we wouldn't chicken out. Or get murdered or something."

And when Dad said "get murdered," his eyes narrowed just like Boris's had when I'd seen him at Lily Putt's.

"But you didn't exactly go in there alone," I said.

"No. Oscar came with me," Dad said.

And I continued my fishing expedition. "Um. The *Yodeler* said that you and Oscar weren't alone either."

Then I saw Dad's cheeks turn red. I'd never thought anything in the world could embarrass my kilt-wearing father, but I had just stumbled onto a serious weakness of his: a weakness named *Linda Swineshead*.

"Oh yeah!" Dad was beaming, obviously overacting surprise. "A girl came with us too! I think her name was something like Linda. Linda Swineshead! Gosh! I haven't thought about Oscar and Linda in decades! Ha ha!"

Then Karim stepped in with his bad-cop interrogation. "Mr. Abernathy, the newspaper said Linda Swineshead was your girlfriend."

Dad looked embarrassed.

I checked the door and window—still closed. It was getting harder to breathe.

And let me say this, too: not only is it impossible for a kid who's just finished eighth grade to imagine his father as an eighth grader, but no one ever wants to think about their dad having long-concealed romantic interests that weren't also his mom.

Dad cleared his throat. "Oh. Uh. Well, that's just—Hey! I thought you boys wanted to hear about going inside the Purdy House. It's a pretty wild story, guys!"

Then Dad got up and switched off the light in my room like he was setting the stage for a scary story around the campfire, except Mom would get really mad if Dad lit a fire on my floor, and my window was also closed, which not only would have caused a campfire to asphyxiate us, but I was already feeling claustrophobic after Dad had shut the door.

"Dad? Would you mind opening the window, please?" I said.

"Oh. Oops. Sorry, Sam."

Then Dad slid my window open and sat back down at the foot of my bed.

"Well, I'm not going to lie, boys. Like most people who live here, the Purdy House gives me the creeps, and to be honest, I never want to go back inside that place," Dad said.

Karim fired an *I told you so* look at me. I hadn't yet told Dad that I was supposed to go inside *that place* the next day.

Dad continued, "And we couldn't get out once we were inside. The basement window we'd come in through was too high to reach."

"You should have tried other doors," Karim said.

"We tried every door and window in the place."

"Even the windows up in the attic?" Karim asked.

Dad nodded. "Even the attic." Then he lowered his voice and said, "It was like the house knew we were inside it and it wasn't going to let us go."

Now I was interested, but also a little scared. I tried to concentrate on what I was going to cook for the Monster People—Boris and Mr. and Mrs. Blank—tomorrow for dinner.

"What was in the attic?" I asked.

"Probably nothing," Dad said. "It was too dark to see, but Oscar swore he stepped on some bones in there, and that was when we heard this faraway screaming and what sounded like singing coming from down below."

Then Dad chuckled nervously. "Oscar and I got pretty scared. One of us screamed. I'm pretty sure it was Oscar, I think. Linda told us to calm down, that it was probably just

Kenny Jenkins[62] and the other boys outside trying to mess with us."

And Dad went on, "So we followed Linda back downstairs. Oscar and I were so scared, we didn't have our eyes open. We held hands all the way back to the main floor, where we all tried the front door again, but the knob wouldn't even turn, like it was welded shut or something. And the howling and music from below seemed to get louder and louder until—"

"Until *what*?" I asked.

"Until Linda opened the basement door again. Then everything went completely silent. Ha ha! Who knows? Maybe it was just a random coincidence. But when we got back down into the basement, that was when Linda found this little door that had to have been less than two feet tall, and it was also the only door in the whole entire place that we could actually open!"

"But the newspaper article—and you—said that Oscar was the one who found the door," I said.

"Well, it was Linda. But we all climbed inside, which was probably not the smartest thing I've ever done," Dad said. "Actually, the only reason all three of us went in was because Oscar and I didn't want to be left behind in that basement all alone."

"Where did the doorway lead to?" Karim asked.

---

[62] Kenny Jenkins had *played football*? This was something I'd need to find out more about.

"It was really spooky. There was a tunnel that had been dug in the dirt—like something you'd see in an old movie about breaking out of jail or something. It gives me claustrophobia just thinking about it."

It suddenly got really quiet in my room, and then Dad cleared his throat and said, "Er. Sorry, Sam."

And now I was beginning to feel claustrophobic just because of Dad's story.

"Oscar got stuck in the tunnel and couldn't go forward or squeeze his way back out. He was pretty big, but when he got stuck there, Linda and I were trapped inside this creepy room that had a coffin in the middle of the floor, and what looked like a table where someone had been playing cards."

"Wait. There was an *actual* coffin? And a card game?" I asked.

"I know. Crazy," Dad said. "But the main thing is that Linda and I were trapped. I tried pushing Oscar's face back, but he was jammed tight. I guess I started to panic, and that's when Linda told me to look out because there was an armadillo in there, and he was running right at me."

I felt myself getting jealous again, and not only because Dad had had a girlfriend named Linda Swineshead, but that armadillo had to have been Bartleby—the same armadillo who'd looked out for me when I'd been trapped in the well, the same armadillo who'd brought me into that very room where Cecilia Pixler-Purdy had stowed the coffin of her first husband, the bank robber Ethan Pixler, just to keep him quiet and stop Little Charlie from continually digging him up, the same armadillo who'd insisted I had a crush on Bahar (but he was wrong about that) just the other day at the Uniontown Mall when I didn't have on any pants.

"And that was all it took. Oscar was so terrified of armadillos that he bit my hand and started screaming. But he slithered out of that little tunnel faster than a greased rattlesnake! And I don't mind saying that Linda and I never looked back one time. When we ran back upstairs—and this is the weirdest part—thousands of bats started coming up from somewhere down below in the basement, and flying out through the chimney. It was the worst thing imaginable. Oscar got so scared, he started to cry. Then we turned around." And Dad paused here, his eyes as big and round as silver dollar coins as he looked back and forth from me to Karim.

He said, "And that's when we noticed that the front door was suddenly wide open, like the house had opened itself up just for us! It was the strangest thing ever; like a scene out of a horror movie or something, except it was all real and happening to us right there. So we made a dash for the outside, and ended up running straight into Sheriff Glick, who drove Oscar and Linda to their homes, but took me to jail—in handcuffs— because he couldn't get a hold of anyone at home. And I'm not afraid to say that I'd *never* go back inside that place. Not *ever*. So if any of your friends get it into their heads that full moons and foolish dares equal fun and games at the Purdy House, well, it's probably time for some new friends."

"Um. Dad? I think there's something Karim and I need to tell you," I said.

"Keep me out of it," Karim said. "And you'd just better hope it's not a full moon tomorrow night."

Dad looked at me, his eyebrows pinched together like he was trying to untie an impossible knot with the tip of his nose.

MY DAD'S FIRST GIRLFRIEND

Everyone in Blue Creek assumed the Purdy House was still just as vacant—and just as haunted—as it had been for more than a century.

But the Blanks had lived in the old house for nearly a week. They had been seen around town looking for shop space for their dead-stuffed-animal emporium, as well as at Lily Putt's Indoor-Outdoor Miniature Golf Complex eating Little Charlie's Haunted Burgers and getting quadruple bogeys[63] on the llama hole, but it was like they might as well have been invisible to anyone in town except for me, Bahar, and Karim.

I didn't get it.

Maybe they really *were* some kind of Monster People.

Dad was mad at me for accepting the catering job from them. He told me no son of an Abernathy would ever step foot inside the Purdy House, and said he was going to talk to Mom about it. But I didn't really believe him since *talking to Mom* meant that he'd probably have to confront his past, which

---

[63] That's a really bad score.

would most likely involve an explanation about the whole Linda Swineshead thread to his story.

It was Friday, and there was so much going on in my brain. I had to go shopping and get things ready for the dinner at the Blanks' (because no matter what Dad said, turning down a chef job was off the table), I still needed to return *Princess Snugglewarm versus the Charm School Dropouts* to the library, and James Jenkins would be coming this weekend to spend the last few moments of freedom and summer vacation with me.

There was so much here, and so much I'd be saying good-bye to.

And that included Blue Creek, too, so the insomniac spiders on trampolines in my stomach had been bouncing around like a million off-balance washing machines. I tried to stay calm by focusing on unsweetened iced tea with Bahar at Colonel Jenkins' Diner, because that was coming on Saturday too.

Like I said, I had an awful lot to think about.

In the morning, Mom drove me and Karim to the grocery store so I could pick up the ingredients for the Boris-and-his-parents-and-Bahar dinner. Karim complained after half an hour because I was taking too long, walking up and down the aisles and trying to conjure up recipes, but everything I thought about making seemed to whisper to me, *Boris is going to hate that, and he will make you feel awful for trying to serve it to him.* I finally decided to do a chicken-tarragon potpie with an upside-down blood orange cake for dessert.

Everyone likes chicken potpies, right? Maybe even Boris, I thought.

But it was when we were driving back home after dropping *Princess Snugglewarm* off at the library[64] that Mom made a random Mom comment that nearly gave me a panic attack.

To be honest, it *did* give me a panic attack.

She said this: "Linda called me this morning and said she'd be dropping James off tomorrow afternoon at about four, so make sure you're back from whatever you have planned for your last Saturday in Blue Creek."

Linda?

And *last Saturday*? Surely Mom had miscalculated. I still had two more Saturdays, or so I thought. Mom had to be wrong.

"Linda?" I said.

"Oh! Ha ha. Mrs. Jenkins. You know, James's mom. Linda."

I'd never known that James's mom's first name was Linda.

But I'd heard or read the name "Linda" at least a hundred times in the last day or so, and it was starting to traumatize me. Still, "Linda" was a common name, right? There had to be at least four or five Lindas who'd lived in Blue Creek.

And were approximately my dad's age.

Right?

---

[64] Also, I might add, just seeing books was making me feel guilty for not getting my summer reading done. Or started. And I knew there was going to be a blurry-eyed marathon of page-turning coming up for me very soon.

ANDREW SMITH

I glanced back at Karim, who was sitting alone in the backseat with the groceries. His expression showed that he was thinking the same thing I was, and sure enough, Karim, never at a loss for words or saltiness, said, "You'd think she'd change back to her maiden name after how long the Jenkinses have been divorced."

"I think she wanted to," Mom said. "But it's so hard to get used to. I mean, calling her 'Linda Swineshead' again after all these years. So you boys better mind yourselves and be nice if she stays for a bit. Be sure to ask her if she wants you to call her 'Miss Swineshead.' I bet she'd like that. It's the polite thing to do—the Texas thing to do."

This was almost too much to bear.

James Jenkins's mother used to be my dad's *girlfriend*.

And naturally Karim, who was working on getting evicted from my room, and possibly walking home along the side of the highway, continued: "Hmm . . . *Linda Swineshead*. That name sounds familiar."

I whirled around and gave my friend an *I'm going to kick you out and make you go back to live next door to the Purdy House with your sunburned nudist parents* look, which I knew he understood.

Mom said, "Does it?"

Karim, as cool as ice, said, "Yeah. There's a character in one of the books Sam and I are reading for his summer work named 'Linda Cowspleen,' who's a junior high history teacher with a time travel machine, and she sends all her worst students back to ancient Greece to do battle with that one guy with the octopus growing out of his face."

"Ooh! That sounds good! I never read that one!" Mom said.

"You should ask Sam about it when we get to the end," Karim added. "It's a real page-turner!"

And I wanted to shout at Karim, *There is NOT that one guy with an octopus growing out of his face—not anywhere in the collected literary accomplishments of mankind!*

But instead I said this: "Mom? You said this would be my last Saturday in Blue Creek. I thought we weren't leaving for another week after that. Right? We're not leaving that soon, are we?"

Mom reached across and patted my knee the way you'd pat the head of a small dog who was scared of fireworks or something.

"Well, James's mother is going to be in Albuquerque with her sister, so we said we'd drive him along with us to New Mexico. We thought you'd enjoy having a friend along for part of the trip so it wouldn't be so scary for you. Dad says we should leave on Monday. Won't that be fun?"

No, I thought, it would not be fun to leave more than an *entire week* early. Not fun at all.

And now the spiders were trying to climb up through my neck.

Karim added, "You mean *Miss Swineshead* is going to be in Albuquerque. Right, Mrs. Abernathy?"

I had never punched anyone in my life, but I really wanted to sock Karim at that point.

I said, "I think you'd better pull the car over, Mom. I feel like I'm going to be sick."

SWALLOWED BY A HUNGRY CIRCUS TENT

"**Anyone who ever spent the shortest amount of time with** that awful little Boris Blank is definitely going to avoid having anything to do with children for the rest of their life," I said.

Karim gave his cousin a serious look. "I guess this means you're never going to be a teacher, mother, or pediatrician now," he said.

It was Friday afternoon, and Karim and Bahar were at my house, keeping me company while I prepared the meal I was catering for Boris and his parents. Well, Karim wasn't keeping me company so much as he was establishing permanent legal residency in my home and getting to the point where even my parents would be unable to have him evicted. Not that they would ever want to.

And Karim went on, "Or a clown who makes balloon sculptures at birthday parties, someone who gives Shetland pony rides at the fairgrounds, or a miniature golf course owner."

I rolled my eyes. I knew what Karim was getting at with his "miniature golf course" reference, but I wasn't going to argue with him, because I *did not* have a crush on Bahar.

Karim said, "Face it. That Boris kid is a ruiner of people's lives."

"Boris isn't that bad," Bahar said.

"He takes baths in milk and Diet Coke. You told me he almost made you cry," Karim argued.

Every once in a while, but not too often, Karim was right. I'd talked to Bahar about babysitting for Boris, and it was true that she had nearly cried, which is something Bahar never does. But here I was now, actually putting the finishing touches on a delicious meal for Boris and his parents. And I dreaded the thought of stepping foot inside the Purdy House, so I couldn't stop asking my brain what my mouth had gotten me into.

"All I can say is, they must pay you pretty good for just sitting there with him, trying to keep him entertained when all he does is make you feel inadequate as he's contemplating eating you, which is exactly what Little Charlie would have done," Karim said.

"I don't think there was any such thing as babysitters in the 1800s," I pointed out.

"Any kid who's been raised by wolves probably doesn't need a babysitter, anyway," Bahar said.

And Karim said, "All I can say is, you're both crazy for agreeing to go inside that house."

"If you were a true friend, you'd come along and help with dinner so we could both keep Bahar company. You could be a server with me," I said. "And you never know. Maybe you'll end up being the only human on the planet that Boris actually likes."

Bahar added, "Or doesn't want to eat."

"Sorry, but I've made other plans for tonight," Karim said.

"What plans are those?" Bahar asked.

"Um. I'm reading a book. It's about a guy with an octopus growing out of his face," Karim said.

"That sounds like a great book," Bahar said unenthusiastically. Then she added, "You know who'd probably like to help out, Sam? Brenden Saltarello. He told me he'd give anything to have a look inside the actual Purdy House."

I couldn't tell if Bahar was teasing or not, but Karim gave me a look like he'd just been stabbed in the heart by his cousin. But Brenden Saltarello must have been crazy if he actually wanted to go inside the Purdy House for no reason outside of just seeing what it was like.

"Well, he's not afraid of mayonnaise, so I'd bet he's not afraid of cannibalistic wolf boy ghosts, either. Does he have a white button-up shirt?" I asked.

When you're a professional caterer, the outfit counts.

Karim looked genuinely stung when Bahar said, "I'll text him and ask."

The chicken-tarragon potpie was nearly finished; the blood orange upside-down cake was cooling, and I was just about to put my herbed Persian Salad-e Shirazi in the refrigerator to chill.

ANDREW SMITH

And while Bahar texted (or pretended to text) Brenden, Karim leaned closer to me and whispered, "She wouldn't really do that to me, would she?"

I didn't honestly know if Bahar would do something like try to make Karim jealous, but, as she'd said, *someone definitely had a crush on someone*, so I just shrugged and gave Karim a palms-up *I don't know* look.

Anyway, Karim deserved it. He'd been taking every opportunity to torment me and Bahar about anything he could.

I said, "Hey! Just think, Bahar—if it's me, you, and Brenden in the Purdy House tonight, it'll be just like my dad; James's mom, Mrs. Jenkins . . . er, Miss Swineshead; and Oscar Padilla on a night from twenty-something years ago."

And then I immediately regretted saying it because my dad and Linda Swineshead had been boyfriend and girlfriend (and I did *not* have a crush on Bahar). Plus I was terrified that something like what had happened to those three kids so many years ago might actually happen to us. But I didn't like teasing Karim about things like that, so I felt bad for my friend, and also terrified for me and Bahar (and possibly for Brenden Saltarello if Bahar actually was talking—or texting—him into coming along). And I especially didn't want to end up being arrested and going to jail, like my dad had.

Bahar said, "Brenden *does* have a white shirt. He said he'd love to go there with us tonight and he'll be here in twenty minutes."

Karim looked like he'd been punched in the stomach.

A few months ago, when I'd first posted my catering and dining jobs flyer in the library's Teen Zone, I'd bought a white chef's jacket and some houndstooth-patterned pants, with money I'd saved up from working at Lily Putt's. And although the outfit was too big for me, I was thrilled for any opportunity that came along where I'd get to dress like a real chef.

The sleeves on my double-breasted jacket were rolled up to my elbows, and my pants were cuffed at least five times because they just didn't make chef uniforms in boys' size M. I'd have to change that, I thought. There were enough square yards of clothes fabric around my body to easily contain two or three Sam Abernathy–size chefs.

"That chef's outfit makes you look fat, Sam," Karim thoughtfully pointed out. He was pouting about Brenden.

"It looks like he's been swallowed by a hungry circus tent," Bahar said.

We heard the sound of slamming car doors, and then the ring of the doorbell. Brenden Saltarello, looking like a professional waiter, dressed in a white, tucked-in collared shirt and the kind of shoes you'd wear to a wedding, was at the front door.

And Karim dashed away down the hall to hide in my (his) bedroom.

ANDREW SMITH

PART FOUR
BYE-BYE, BLUE CREEK

WHAT EVERYONE NEEDS TO KNOW ABOUT THE MONSTER PEOPLE (PART 6)

What Everyone Needs to Know about the Monster People:

✔ Have not been seen in daylight. May be vampires.

✔ Have a lamp made out of a dead raccoon.

✔ Have a hideous black flying beast that is bulletproof and comes out of their house at night during all the screaming.

✔ Have a coffin buried fifty feet below the ground to keep the Wolf Boy from digging it up again.

✔ Have a kid named Boris.

✔ May be transforming Bahar into a mindless thrall with no will of her own.

✔ Boris absorbs nutrients through his skin in his bathwater.

✔ They have now begun an indoctrination spell on Sam.

✔ ~~SAM IS NOT ALLOWED TO TELL JOKES TO BRENDEN SALTARELLO EVER AGAIN!!!~~

✔ Their last name is BLANK.

✔ What is Sam thinking, going over there and inviting Brenden Saltarello along???

✔ If Sam, Bahar, and Brenden never come back after tonight, I'm moving into Sam's room for good.

AS MUTE AS A MECHANICAL LLAMA

"One thing to remember: if that horrible child asks you to tell him the ingredients in the chicken potpie, or what kind of dressing is on the salad, or what a blood orange is, just smile and nod like you can't understand English or something," I said.

Brenden, Bahar, and I stood outside the intimidating, spike-studded iron gates of the Purdy House with a wheeled cart containing all the food and settings for my latest professionally catered event. But it was almost like none of us wanted to be the person initially responsible for actually touching and then opening the portal to the most haunted house in Texas.

Karim was nowhere to be found. He'd been hiding in my room ever since Brenden had showed up at my house, probably inside my closet looking for clean clothes or something. I don't know if he was more afraid of the Purdy House or of having to be face-to-face with Brenden Saltarello.

I went on, "And Bahar will back me up on this: the only reason Boris ever wants to talk to you is to make you feel bad, or to tell you how much he hates things, so trust me, you're better off just not saying anything at all to him, not one word, because once he tricks you into answering a question, it's almost like he can take control of your mind or something."

Brenden Saltarello looked at Bahar and then shifted his eyes to me.

He said, "He's six years old, right? You're messing with me, Sam."

Bahar shook her head. "No. That pretty much describes Boris exactly."

"Well, I've got to see this," Brenden said.

Then Brenden Saltarello reached out and lifted the latch on the old iron gate and pushed the gate open.

The giant gate made a sound like a super-screechy cat being stepped on by a super-big foot in super-slow motion. For some reason all three of us inhaled at the same time.

And before I knew what was happening, I was inside the grounds of the Purdy House. I felt a little dizzy—not claustrophobia dizzy, just *dizzy*. I wheeled the cart up to the front steps, and Brenden helped me lift it up onto the porch. Now my actual feet[65] were touching the wooden planks of the actual Purdy House's front porch. I glanced back over my shoulder in the direction of the woods—where Sam's Well would be—and past that, in the direction of the normal and not-haunted part of Blue Creek.

---

[65] Well, my shoes, with my feet inside them.

194   ANDREW SMITH

There was no turning back now.

"Okay. This place is really creepy," Brenden whispered.

And we weren't even inside the house yet.

We didn't get a chance to knock, or to ring whatever horrifying-sounding bell might be installed on the house, because the door swung open with an enthusiastic swish that made us all jump slightly. And standing there was the Blank family—Timmy, Beth, and behind them in the dim shadows of the house's interior lurked little unpleasant Boris.

"Well, well, well! Thank you for being here on time," Timmy Blank said. Then he looked at Brenden as though he was trying to remember if he'd been expecting him or not.

I cleared my throat. "Ahem. This is Brenden. He's part of the waitstaff for Catering by Sam," I said, suddenly lying as effortlessly as Karim ever did, since Catering by Sam had never existed before the words had come out of my mouth, and there definitely were no employees besides myself, which meant I'd probably need to pay Brenden some of the money I made from the Blanks.

"Nice to meet you, Brenden!" Beth Blank said. "Don't you boys look like perfect culinary artists!"

Maybe I was just nervous, but the way she said it made it sound like we were the meal and not the servers of it.

"Come in! Come in!" Timmy Blank said, and he stood at the open doorway and held an arm extended back into the depths of the Purdy House. That was when Boris walked right up to Brenden, put his face just about three inches in front of the third button on Brenden's shirt, and said, "What did you guys make us for dinner?"

But I was too fast for Boris. I intercepted his torpedo before it could get anywhere near to sinking the SS *Saltarello*.

I waved my hand between Boris and Brenden and said, "Oh. He never talks. Not at all. It is seen as unprofessional in the fine catering business, so you may as well not say anything to Brenden for the rest of the night. He's as mute as the mechanical llama at Lily Putt's!"

"So impressive!" Beth Blank said. Then she added, "Here, let me show you boys where to go."

And just like that I stepped forward, pulling the cart behind me, crossing over the threshold and into the musty and cool interior of the Purdy House.

HUNDREDS OF EYES

Someone—anyone—should have given Timmy and Beth Blank a few pointers on how to effectively decorate a home so that it feels welcoming and inviting, as opposed to ghastly and horrifying.

Walking into the downstairs living room felt like walking out onto a stage in front of an enormous audience. There were so many eyes looking at me—maybe hundreds of them—and they were all unblinking, pointed into the center of the room, black and frozen in expressions of rage, astonishment, and fear.

And they were all dead.

I saw a wild pig with a pipe in his mouth wearing an old German hiking hat, standing on the hearth of the stone fireplace, over which hung an enormous wooden plaque with the snarling head of a bear and his two disembodied front feet with claws unnaturally spread open like he was making "jazz hands" at us; a grinning alligator that had been turned into a glass-topped coffee table; a python with its mouth open in some kind of gruesome, frozen, hissing bite, that was coiled around the bottom of a potted plant;[66] a mother skunk, out for a stroll along the baseboards, followed by three tiny baby skunks that looked like photocopies of each other; a couple of decapitated deer and elk; a smiling Siamese house cat with a starched ball of yarn unraveling between its claws; a large snapping turtle standing up on its hind legs,[67] eyes and mouth wide, front arms arched like a boxer's, in some kind of bizarre fight with a koala bear, like in one of those cheesy old dinosaur movies where a brontosaurus and a stegosaurus square off at the edge of a cliff; hawks, vultures, owls, blue jays, ducks, pheasants hanging in petrified flight; and in one corner, standing on a round end table next to an old wingback chair upholstered in zebra skin, was the notorious raccoon lamp, even more hideous up close than I might have ever dreamed, and yes, one of its hind legs had lost all its fur.

The raccoon lamp was also wearing little wire-framed glasses and a miniature sailor's cap, and it was posed with both of its arms up in the air, like it was in the process of being arrested or something.

It was all so terrifying, and so incredibly *weird*.

After spending one night there babysitting, Bahar must have already gotten used to the decor inside the Purdy House, but Brenden looked at me, his eyes wide and the corners of his mouth turned down as though he was considering that we had been transported into an actual horror show.

---

[66] There was a taxidermied rat with a distinctive *Oh my!* expression on his little rat face stretched across the snake's tongue.
[67] And turtles do NOT stand like that.

There were just so many unmoving eyes, and so many rows of exposed teeth. I never realized animals could snarl as much as the ones inside the Purdy House did.

"Sorry about all the clutter," Mr. Blank said. "We plan on moving most of our babies into the shop, once we find one, that is!"

And I thought, *Did he just call them his babies?*

Mrs. Blank took us into the dining room (more eyes and teeth) and the kitchen, which seemed to be the designated room for housing mounted and lacquered dead fish (so you usually only saw one eye at a time),[68] and left us on our own to assemble the evening meal.

Naturally Boris, who was both fascinated and challenged by the nonspeaking Brenden, never stayed more than a few inches away from him.

"Hey, kid." Boris tugged on Brenden Saltarello's perfectly white, creased shirtsleeve. "Hey, you. Kid. Hey. Hey."

"He doesn't talk," I reminded Boris. "Just think of him as something you'd have mounted on your wall."

But that was no deterrent to Boris, who continued his tugging and pestering, while Brenden gave me an *I don't want to be a thing on their wall* look.

---

[68] Think about it—fish have an eye on each side of their head, so you usually only see one eye. The exception was a lone gar fish that was mounted (just its head and about one third of its body) coming straight out of the wall, mouth wide open and filled with dozens of glistening needlelike teeth.

"Hey. Hey, kid. Hey. What's your name again?"

"Brenden. His name is Brenden," I said. "But he doesn't talk."

Brenden Saltarello unpacked the place settings and carried them out into the dining room, Boris practically attached to his elbow. It was pretty impressive, because not only did Brenden refuse to break under Boris's relentless pestering, but he knew exactly how to set a proper table too.

"Hey. Hey, kid. Hey, Brenden. After dinner, do you want to go play down in the basement?" Boris said.

Horrifying.

I said, "No, he does not."

I had all the food out, and began putting the final touches on the presentation. It was almost time to serve. Bahar lit candles in the dining room. Everything was as perfect as it would have been if we were being photographed for one of those fancy food magazines, except for how badly my chef's uniform fit, and all the horrible dead creatures that were everywhere in the house. There was even a small bobcat in the centerpiece of the dining table that was missing an eye and had its mouth forever stretched back in a ridiculously wide yawn, or maybe it was trying really hard to cough up an uncooperative hair ball. The bobcat's front paws had little brackets on them that held salt and pepper shakers.

Who would ever eat salt and pepper from the paws of a one-eyed choking dead bobcat?

ANDREW SMITH

I continued, "Brenden doesn't talk, and he doesn't play in basements, either."

Boris was un-swayed.

"Hey. Hey, Brenden, have you ever had to hide inside a dumpster in order to get away from a hungry mountain lion?"

Brenden Saltarello didn't need to say anything. He just gave me a look that said, *Please make this kid go away.*

"Hey. Hey, kid. Hey, kid named Brenden who doesn't talk. If you tell me just one thing, I promise I'll leave you alone for a little while," Boris said.

And even Bahar tried running interference on Boris, but it didn't work. She said, "Oh, Boris. Why don't you go tell your parents they can sit at the table now? Sam's just about ready to serve dinner."

"You're the babysitter," Boris said. "And that Brenden guy who doesn't talk is the helper boy. Do you all think it's fair for the two of you to make me do *your* work like that? Are you trying to trick me into leaving or something? You hate me, don't you? You probably hate all children—except for that kid boyfriend of yours who wears a skirt sometimes when he's not dressed in giant man clothes that don't fit and cooks disgusting stuff that nobody would ever eat and then tries to call it food."

Now Boris had gone too far on multiple levels.

It's not a *skirt*; it's a kilt.

And I was *not* Bahar's *boyfriend.*

Also, Boris was still pinching the sleeve of Brenden's shirt between his thumb and index finger.

Bahar nervously ahem-ed and then said, "I'll go call Mr. and Mrs. Blank."

"Let go of Brenden, and I'll tell you what we're having for dinner," I said, with no intention at all of telling Boris what I had actually prepared. And Brenden looked like a fish who'd just spit out a hook and jumped off the line when Boris released his sleeve.

"Okay. I did it. What are we having?" Boris asked.

I pulled a chair out. "Here. Have a seat."

Boris sat, and I wondered if there was any duct tape or rope lying around, but then I thought that things like tying up kids would probably be bad for Bahar's future business.

So I said, "Tonight I've prepared a pappardelle with duck breast, mustard, and juniper berries."[69]

Boris's face mimicked the hair-ball-coughing one-eyed bobcat's.[70]

Then he said this: "That sounds really great!"

What an awful child. What a horrible thing to say.

"Well, of course it does," I said.

"I thought you said it was chicken potpie," said Brenden, who'd obviously forgotten that he didn't talk.

"Does that have chicken in it?" Boris asked. "I hate chicken. I hate pie."

---

[69] As far as I know, this dish does not exist. But I thought it sounded like something I might try.

[70] Except for the fact that Boris had both of his eyes.

If there was a portal to the underworld in the Purdy House, Brenden Saltarello had just opened it, I thought.

Thankfully, before all the demons of Hades could escape, Bahar came in, followed by Mr. and Mrs. Blank.

THE SECRET EATER

No one among us had ever expected the things that would happen that night at the Purdy House.

Throughout the dinner, Boris sat with his lower lip poked out and his arms crossed tightly, staring at his meal as though lasers were about to fire from his eyes and vaporize the entire table.

Beth Blank said, "This is the best meal I've had in ages!"

I felt myself blushing. Brenden and I stood quietly by the entrance to the kitchen like some kind of dinner sentries. It would have been unforgivable for either of us to actually eat in front of the clients.

And at some point, Beth Blank turned to Bahar with a serious look on her face and said, "Boris likes to play tricks on babysitters. Just so you know, he is *not* allowed to take baths in milk or Mountain Dew, cottage cheese, or canned pork-and-beans."

He's taken baths in cottage cheese and canned pork-and-beans? I thought.

"Knowing this will make things a lot easier," Bahar said.

That would be a lot of cans of beans to open too.

So Timmy and Beth Blank thanked me and Brenden one more time after dinner, which Boris sat through but did not eat, and then they left to go into Blue Creek while Brenden and I cleaned up. But a few times during the meal, Beth Blank made excuses for Boris's *eccentric*[71] behavior: "Don't feel bad about Boris, Sam. He's a very fussy eater. Most nights, I'll wake up at two or three in the morning only to hear him rummaging around in the house, looking for food."

I bet you do, I thought.

"Boris is a *secret eater*," Timmy Blank said, and when he said "secret eater," he winked at me.

I wondered how many secrets Boris had eaten in his little six-year-old life.

So it was just when Brenden and I had finished packing things up to haul back home (where Karim was still hiding and pouting, probably) that Bahar called out to us from somewhere in the maze of rooms inside the Purdy House.

"Sam? Brenden? I can't find Boris, and there are bats coming out of the fireplace!"

Brenden looked at me, eyes wide, with an expression that almost asked if maybe the Purdy House was like a sanctuary for wandering vampires, which, if it was, that part of the story had never been reported in the *Hill Country Yodeler*.

---

[71] Sometimes people use words like "eccentric" because it's nicer than saying "annoying" or "repulsive."

Brenden and I went out into the living room, but it was already getting too dark to see.

"This is creepy," Brenden whispered.

"I'll turn on the raccoon," I said.

And that was when the first very strange thing happened—or *seemed* to happen.[72]

I found a little switch on the electrical cord coming out of the raccoon[73] that turned on the bulb poking through the sailor's cap, and out of the poor, bald-legged creature's skull, and when the light came on, I noticed that the raccoon seemed to be standing in a different position, with his arms crossed in front of his little chest,[74] and the raccoon's tiny wire-framed glasses were now missing.

And when the light came on, I also saw something that was engraved on a small brass plate on the wooden base beneath the raccoon's hind legs that said this:

ISHMAEL (1885–1891)

BELOVED PET AND COMPANION

No wonder Ishmael's leg was bald—he was almost one hundred fifty years old.

---

[72] To be honest, it wasn't the *first*, but it was one of those Purdy House–type things that nobody was expecting.

[73] In a place where you wouldn't ever want an electrical cord coming out of.

[74] The same way Boris had been sitting during dinner.

ANDREW SMITH

Also, something struck me as odd and familiar about the raccoon's name, but I couldn't quite remember what it was.

Bahar stood near the fireplace and the wild pig in the hiking hat, who also seemed to have been strangely repositioned into a running pose. And the bear head above the mantel was different too. Its former "jazz hands" had been transformed into two enthusiastic bear thumbs-up, as though he were sincerely approving of our performance. Bahar held on to the little ash broom from the fireplace set, and waved it toward the ceiling, where—yes—two bats were flying around and around, making absolutely no sound at all outside the occasional thumps and thuds produced by fluttering into the walls.

"We need to open some windows!" Brenden said, but the first one he tried—the one behind the sofa where the mother skunk had been parading her stuffed babies, who all seemed to have magically migrated to the opposite side of the room—would not move an inch.

"It's stuck," he said.

The bats kept circling wildly, battering themselves against the walls as Bahar tried to sweep them away.

Brenden tried another window, but like the first one, it wouldn't budge. In fact, none of the windows in the entire downstairs of the Purdy House was functional.

Thump! Thump! went the bats.

"Hey! The koala bear is different!" Bahar said.

Sure enough, the koala bear (the one that had been posed

in a fistfight with the snapping turtle) had moved. The snapping turtle was now turned onto its back, and the koala was straddling the underside of its shell, one little koala hand grasping the turtle's neck and the other clenched in a fist, about to punch the turtle square in the face.

And the snapping turtle had an expression that seemed to say, *Did I say something wrong?*

I guess koala bears and snapping turtles just naturally hate each other.

At least I had finally found something here in Blue Creek that I was not going to mind saying good-bye to at all: the Purdy House.

"Try opening the front door," I said to Brenden as the bats continued to circle and thud, circle and thud.

I suppose we all started to panic when Brenden announced that the front door was stuck shut. Well, when I say "we all," I pretty much mean me and Brenden.

Bahar never panicked about anything.

But we were trapped inside the Purdy House, just like my dad, Linda Swineshead, and his friend Oscar Padilla had been trapped there all those years before. And to make matters worse, Boris was hiding or missing, and just when Brenden had told us that the door to the outside and the usually sane part of Blue Creek was hopelessly jammed, we'd heard the faintest sound like singing coming up through the air from somewhere far below our feet.

We all froze, held our breath, and listened. It sounded like

ANDREW SMITH

a chorus of voices, but a hundred miles away. We couldn't make out what exactly was being sung to us, and the bats continued their tireless crashing into the walls, which was actually louder than the music.

Brenden and I both screamed when something said, "I'm up in the attic!" even though the something that said it was up in the attic happened to be a six-year-old boy named Boris Blank. Still, just the thought of being inside that horrible Purdy House with all those stuffed dead animals that seemed to move by themselves, bats coming out of the fireplace, music from belowground, and all the doors and windows sealed tight was almost too much to handle.

Bahar seemed unfazed. She held on to the brass fireplace broom and shouted up the stairway, "Boris, come downstairs now!"

"I want to play hide-and-seek," called Boris's ghostly voice from somewhere above (while the singing and bat-thumping continued). "You're supposed to find me, in case you were wondering what kinds of things *real* babysitters do!"

Bahar lowered her ash broom and marched through the foyer toward the staircase.

She said to me, "Remind me to *never* babysit for Boris Blank, ever again."

"I think I could do that," I said.

Brenden rattled the doorknob again, but nothing happened.

And after about five seconds beneath the swirling bats, standing in the middle of all those eyes and the animals that had mysteriously changed positions, I decided I'd rather be upstairs in the attic with Bahar than trapped down here with Brenden and the singing, and all of the Blanks' extremely creepy *babies*.

As I climbed the stairs, I never stopped for a second to consider that attics are always the creepiest part of any creepy house.

THE BRAINS AND BELLIES OF A HAUNTED HOUSE

One does not simply go, unaccompanied, looking for the entrance to the attic of a haunted house.

That was a rule to live by, but unfortunately, it was not one I'd thought about before running upstairs after Bahar.

Attics are like the brains of haunted houses.

I didn't wait to ask if Brenden was coming with me, and I couldn't see or hear Bahar. But when I got up to the third floor of the Purdy House,[75] there were two of those super-creepy pull-down attic ladders at opposite ends of the upper hallway, both of them opened, and they were pointing in opposite directions as though the house had two separate attics.

Two brains.

And I naturally chose the wrong one.

I climbed up.

The room that I reached was very small and very dark. There was no window and no light switch, either. From what

---

[75] The same floor where we had seen little Boris standing at the window wearing a nightshirt in the photograph that Karim had taken just a few days ago, which now seemed like years ago.

little bit of light was coming up through the trapdoor, I could see that along one wall there were shelves cluttered with jars and small boxes, as well as a few pieces that must have been Mr. Blank's "works in progress." Another wall seemed to be the house's main electrical panel, with switches labeled KITCHEN, LIVING ROOM, BASEMENT, and so on.

But it only took me about a second to realize two things: first, this was *not* where Boris and Bahar were; and second, what the (excuse me) heck was I doing inside such a small, dark, windowless room?

I took a deep breath and turned back toward the trapdoor ladder I'd climbed to get there, but I must have grabbed on to the mechanism that releases the catch, because in just a matter of seconds, the ladder retracted and folded upward, closing me inside.

So there I was, all alone in the dark.

And then not alone anymore.

"If attics are the brains of a haunted house, then basements are the bellies!"

A light came on, and I found myself once again face-to-face with an armadillo named Bartleby. Also, I was apparently somewhere else inside the Purdy House, which was not a comforting thought. But I knew I had been there before, and it was all teasing at me, whispering—like a dream that you just can't recall, but you still can somehow sense that it's hiding there, tickling away at your thoughts.

ANDREW SMITH

Then it all came rushing back to me, a memory from when I was four years old and trapped in the hole that would forever come to be known as "Sam's Well"—the broken chair; the woodstove with the hanging and disconnected chimney pipe (which probably explained where Bahar's bats had come from); the playing cards and chest of drawers with the pennies and buttons in it; the twisted, witch-hair-like roots tangling down through the impossibly dark ceiling overhead.

I was back inside Ethan Pixler's secret hideout—the belly of the Purdy House.

"Ah! Remember, Sam? This is where it all began!" Bartleby said, and when he said "all began," he made a graceful rainbow in the air over his head with his stubby front armadillo arms, like a bloom opening up.

"Where *what* all began?" I asked.

Bartleby squinted and pointed his snout to the left, then to the right, and then just for good measure back to the left again. "You know—you and me. Our journey through life together, Sam!"

"Oh. That," I said. "And how did I get here? The last thing I remember is that I was up in an attic in the dark. How did I end up down in this place?"

"Ha ha! Don't you remember? You fell down a hole when you were just about the size of a potato bug!" Bartleby laughed and slapped what would be his knee if armadillos had such things as knees.

Most of the time, Bartleby could be absolutely infuriating. And the rest of the time, he was merely annoying.

"I'm just kidding!" he said. "You followed me here through the secret passageway. No respectable haunted house could ever be built without lots and lots of secret passageways! And it was a lucky thing you needed me too, because I'd never have thought my old pal Ishmael would still be around here, just hanging out—and with a lightbulb sticking out of his noggin to boot! Ha ha! So, thanks for pointing him out to me! And, if I might add, I'm sure the only things that come out of my head are brilliant ideas, as opposed to lightbulbs! Ha ha! Brilliant! Like a light! Get it, Sam?"

Ugh.

Ishmael. The more-than-a-century-old lamp-raccoon with the bald leg.

And of course he'd be a friend of Bartleby's.

Bartleby had mentioned the name Ishmael that day I went to the Uniontown Mall, when Mom had wanted to make me try on all those school clothes.

For so many years, I'd always assumed that Bartleby was just a dream I'd have—something that popped into my head when I had claustrophobia, and then disappeared again once the claustrophobia was over. But there was something else about Bartleby that just had to be real.

"You really are real, aren't you?" I said.

Bartleby scratched at the whiskers under his armadillo chin.

"Is that really a *real* question?" he asked. Then he laughed. "Ha ha! Brilliant! You want to know how I can *really* prove I'm *really real*?"

But the last time Bartleby had tricked me into allowing him to prove he was real, he'd (excuse me) pooped on my foot, and I wasn't about to fall for that again.

"Um. No, thanks," I said. "I believe you."

"Oh. Well, that's nice, Sam. Because I've always believed in you," Bartleby said, and if armadillos could have a hurt look in their eyes, Bartleby had one at just that moment.

I felt bad for hurting his feelings. After all, Bartleby had always been there whenever I'd needed him, even if at times I hadn't thought I did. Even if up until tonight, I'd never really believed in him.

"I'm sorry," I said. "That was mean of me."

"So. Does that mean you want me to prove it?" Bartleby grinned a sharp-toothed armadillo grin.

"No."

"Well, if you're finally giving up on disbelieving what is the honest truth, Sam, then you should probably know that we need to get back to the attic before that Brenden kid calls the police, which—trust me—he is about to do."

It really *was* turning out to be just like what had happened to my dad, James's mother,[76] and Oscar Padilla, and I

---

[76] And I still could not get over the fact that they were boyfriend and girlfriend when they were teenagers.

desperately did *not* want to end up being taken to jail like Dad was.

"So!" Bartleby said. "To the secret tunnel!"

And when Bartleby said "secret tunnel," his eyes widened to the size of shiny black quarters.

"That's it?" I asked.

"What do you mean?"

I was confused, and a little bit scared that this was some kind of final good-bye from Bartleby, and nobody likes good-byes. Nobody.

All these good-byes.

"I thought you needed to tell me something, or something," I said.

Bartleby snickered. "Ha ha! Something, or something, or something really real. Ha ha, Sam! You know all the best words!"

Then came the sound of a distant knocking, and I heard Brenden Saltarello somewhere in the house calling, "Sam! Sam!"

He must have been knocking on the attic door, way up above us.

"Come on, Sam! Follow me!" Bartleby waved me toward the tiny doorway in the dirt floor—the same one where Oscar Padilla had gotten stuck that night he'd taken the dare and stayed here with my dad and Linda Swineshead in the Purdy House.

ANDREW SMITH

Bartleby ducked inside his secret passageway, and then paused for a moment before turning around to look at me. Upstairs, Brenden knocked and knocked, bats flew in a permanent circular holding pattern, Bahar was probably cleaning up pork and beans from the bathtub, and stuffed animals moved around when no one was watching them.

Bartleby said, "I will tell you this, though, and I swear on Ethan Pixler's coffin that it's the truth—that I believe you're going to do just great at the new school, Sam! Think about it. It's everything you've always wanted! And I believe you're going to make lots and lots of friends there, so stop being so scared and get over it. It's time to be brilliant, Sam! And I believe you have a crush on your friend Bahar too, and you should stop being scared of that."

I protested, "I do NOT—"

But Bartleby cut me off with a raised (and dirty) armadillo claw in a gesture of, *Hold it right there, pal.*

He said, "But it doesn't matter at all what I believe, Sam, because all of that—everything—is up to you, and what *you* believe in."

Everything went completely black. Then slashes of light broke a rectangle in the floor. I was back inside the little attic room with all the labeled electrical switches on the wall, and Brenden Saltarello was coming into the attic to look for me.

Brilliant.

PRINCESS SNUGGLEWARM COMES TO TOWN, AND THREE ASTONISHED BOBCATS

Everyone in Blue Creek eventually became big fans of the Purdy House and the plan that Mr. and Mrs. Blank presented to the town council for turning it into the centerpiece of a taxidermy theme park called Blue Creek Land.

As Mr. Blank would later explain, "America has waited long enough for a taxidermy theme park, and Blue Creek is just the place to showcase the wonders of preserving death."

So that had been the plan all along.

They opened up the entire house, even the attic and the secret chamber beneath the basement, despite the occasional mysterious noises, and the unexpected icy breezes.

Ethan Pixler must not have been a sound sleeper.

On the other hand, I did not appreciate the inclusion of the Little Boy in the Haunted Well attraction. As it turned out, the small hill of piled-up debris covering the entrance to Sam's Well was on the Blanks' property too. Go figure.

And I couldn't help but wonder what—or who—Mr. Blank would taxidermy to play the part of four-year-old Sam Abernathy.

But we didn't really start to put together the mystery of what had actually been going on at the Purdy House until the following day—the day *after* that horrible night with Boris, the bats, and Ishmael and all his movable friends.

I should explain.

To begin with, it was a lucky thing for me and my parents that Brenden Saltarello did not end up calling the police that night, even though the next day when my non-terrified mind considered the possible outcomes of a 911 call, there was no logical reason I could think of why I would have ended up in jail like my dad had when he was just about my age.[77]

After Brenden found me in the smaller attic—the "brains" of the haunted house—the four of us (Bahar, Brenden, me, and Boris) climbed out through the second-story window in Boris's bedroom and ran all the way in the dark, past Sam's Well (soon to be the Little Boy in the Haunted Well interactive fun house),[78] and through the woods to my house.

Boris, as anyone who knew him would come to expect, complained the whole way: he hated running in the dark, we were kidnapping him, he didn't like the types of trees we have in Texas, he hated one-story houses (my house, in other words), and—of course—he was hungry, and so he asked if I had anything to eat at my house, but I refused to answer him because

---

[77] Also, I might add, as far as I know, to this day Mom never found out about Dad spending the night in jail, or about the whole Linda-Swineshead-who-is-James-Jenkins's-mother-being-his-first-girlfriend thing, either.

[78] And just thinking about this gives me claustrophobia.

I'd already been trapped inside one small black hole that night, and once was more than enough for me.

The normal, non–Monster People of our group were so shaken by the creepy moving-around dead animals and wild attack-bats[79] that we basically said nothing to each other all night regarding what we'd seen in the Purdy House, as each of us silently tried to sort out exactly what it was that truly *had* happened there—and why. We all looked as pale as Boris's nightshirt, and as wide-eyed as astonished salt-and-pepper-bearing bobcats. But with two eyes.

Mom fell instantly in love with Boris. She said he was the most adorable six-year-old boy she'd ever seen, which made me more than a little jealous. And she even suggested that he might like to become playmates with Dylan and Evie, who had already gone to bed. But when Boris asked Mom what a "playmate" was, I knew she would be in for a long and deeply disappointing conversation.

After all, not all monsters are fifty feet tall with enormous fangs, flames spouting from their nostrils, and an insatiable appetite for human beings. Some could be six-year-old boys wearing nightshirts.

And when Boris asked my mom if there were any snacks in the house, I knew Mom was doomed.

Bahar let Mr. and Mrs. Blank know where we were, and then called them again so they could take her and Boris home,

---

[79] I may be exaggerating here.

but before she left, she swore one more time that she would never, ever babysit for Boris Blank again. And after the Blanks came and picked up Bahar and Boris, Brenden and I discovered the disappearing Karim. He was asleep in his bed, which was in my room that had now become Karim's home away from home.

And he was wearing a set of *my* pajamas.

"Hey! Dang, Karim, you have Princess Snugglewarm pj's? I never knew that!" Brenden said. He looked at Karim with awe and wonder, like this was something about Karim that was too impressive for Brenden to overcome, a possible deal breaker on his being okay with their breakup.

But they weren't Karim's pj's; they were MINE.

Karim yawned and stretched, then looked at me with cold and calculating Karim-is-about-to-drop-a-whopping-lie eyes. He said, "Oh yeah. Princess Snugglewarm is way cooler than Teen Titans or the Houston Astros."

Brenden visibly swooned. "I have those exact same pj's!"

And Karim said, "Are you going to see the Princess Snugglewarm author at the library in the morning? We should totally go there together, Brenden!"

Brenden and Karim locked eyes for at least five silent seconds.

Like Bahar had said, *someone has a crush on someone.*

I grabbed one of my summer reading books from the stack on my dresser and tossed it onto my bed.

"If you guys don't mind, I think I'd better get some home-work done before this summer is totally gone," I said.

Saturday came.

The big day—my last Saturday in Blue Creek, the chance to meet A. C. Messer, unsweetened iced tea with Bahar,[80] the return of James Jenkins, and the "big reveal" of what outfit Karim would choose from MY WARDROBE.

I was a mess, and I'd hardly slept at all. The upside was that I'd managed to read the entire book *Animal Farm*, which was really short and also very sad.

So maybe I would finish all that summer reading after all.

Like all summers, this one had stampeded through town like a runaway weekend.

Mom dropped me off at the library. Bahar was already sit-ting down in the front row of chairs in the Teen Zone, and Karim had left my house before breakfast so he could walk there with Brenden. Trey Hoskins's hair was pink that day, the same color as Princess Snugglewarm's mane, and he looked a little nervous because there were only about a dozen kids in the audience at the library waiting to hear A. C. Messer tell his stories about where Princess Snugglewarm came from, and, hopefully, what we might expect from her in the future.

A dozen kids (including Trey Hoskins) at a library author talk might be a disappointing turnout for a place like Austin or

[80] Who I DID NOT have a crush on, by the way.

Houston, but by Blue Creek standards it was a packed house. Still, Mr. Messer seemed perturbed by the size of the audience, and offered only short sarcastic answers to the few questions he got from the kids in attendance. He wasn't anything like I'd expected, but maybe that's how it is with most famous people when you feel like you already know them before you actually get the chance to meet them face-to-face.

When Brenden Saltarello asked him, "Why did she name her horn 'Betsy'?"

His answer was, "Because it rhymes with 'murder.'"

Like I said, he was sarcastic, and not very nice.

Another kid in the audience stood up and said, "How long does it take you to write a book?"

And A. C. Messer answered, "I write one page every thirty seconds."

Bahar, who was sitting next to me, elbowed my side and whispered, "Ask him a question."

I shook my head. I was too nervous for that.

When Karim, who was wearing my ONE AND ONLY Princess Snugglewarm T-shirt, asked A. C. Messer, "How much money do you get paid for writing a book?"

His answer was this: "Two dollars and twenty-five cents. In Bulgarian currency."[81]

Bahar elbowed me again, but I couldn't talk.

---

[81] The currency in Bulgaria is called the lev. This would be about four of them.

And then Bahar said, "Do you often receive complaints from parents who have to somehow balance the enormous popularity Princess Snugglewarm has among young people with the fact that she is frequently and arbitrarily violent?"

In response, A. C. Messer simply said, "No."

Another elbow from Bahar.

So finally I gathered my strength, swallowed the knot in my throat, raised my hand, and said, "Aioli is a kind of mayonnaise that tastes really good."

I know. It wasn't a question.

But Karim almost immediately blurted out, "I'd like to try aioli!"

And A. C. Messer lifted up his hands like he was begging for some kind of heavenly reprieve and said, "I'm through here."

I suppose artists are known for sometimes being temperamental.

But in his final remarks before allowing us to line up and get Mr. Messer to sign our personal copies of his books, Trey Hoskins mentioned that Mr. Messer had come to Blue Creek as part of a business venture with the new family in town—the Blank family—who were working on developing a robotic-taxidermied-animal theme park with him.

As if that explained everything.

In a matter of seconds, Brenden, Bahar, and I glanced knowingly at each other. It was like a big narration bubble in a Princess Snugglewarm comic had been filled in above our heads, and once again we looked like astonished bobcats who had just figured out the meaning of everything. That was the reason behind the weird moving animals in the Purdy House, and for all those switches on the wall of the small attic where I'd gotten trapped.

I think we simultaneously exhaled sighs of relief, knowing that what had happened to us the night before wasn't as crazy as we'd thought it was, even though it was still pretty crazy.

THE LAST ICED TEA OF SUMMER

Someone should have warned me about how awful it was going to be.

It was impossible to think that anything could be more stomachache-inducing than the feeling of knowing this was the final Saturday of summer, the last time Bahar and I would share an unsweetened iced tea at Colonel Jenkins's Diner in Blue Creek, Texas.

As usual, the place was empty except for the two of us. And it seemed quieter than it had ever been before too.

Kenny Jenkins was just as surly and unwelcoming as ever. He predictably mumbled about how Bahar and I were the only people in the state of Texas who expected him to make tea without adding a five-pound bag of sugar to it, and how things like unsweetened tea were as uncivilized in these parts of the country as boys who didn't like to play football. Kenny Jenkins never did get over the fact that James gave up on his father's dream of football stardom so that he could go live with his mother in Austin and do what he wanted to do most of all, which was dance. And I'm sure Kenny Jenkins blamed me more than anyone else for the changes in his son.

And the thing that was even more frustrating to me was that Bahar and I didn't talk about things the way we always had before. It was as though the pressure of this being my last Saturday in Blue Creek had somehow taken all the air out of the room and left us wordless. There was a lot that I wanted to say, but I didn't want Bahar to feel bad for me.

The spiders hadn't stopped running laps in my stomach for days. They weren't just running laps; now they were also beating drums and setting off fireworks. The truth is, I was afraid of leaving home, even if I didn't really like Blue Creek and everything it had been to me for my entire life. I had nothing else to compare Blue Creek to. Maybe Oregon would be nothing but endless abandoned wells to fall into.

And maybe James was right that there was something wrong with me, but maybe it wasn't about Bahar, like he'd told me it was. Maybe it was about Blue Creek.

Maybe it was about facing all those good-byes.

"I guess we both must be exhausted after what happened last night," Bahar said.

"What do you mean?" I asked.

"Well. You're not saying much," she said. "I detect the presence of an elephant in the room, Sam."

"Maybe it walked over here from the Purdy House. Is it taxidermied and robotic?"

Bahar smiled, which momentarily seemed to increase the level of oxygen in the air.

I swirled my straw around in my tea, trying to fish out a lemon seed.

I said, "I'm just trying to get this lemon seed out of my tea."

Swirl.

Swirl.

Lemon seeds are really hard to catch with a straw.

"You know what's a great idea?" I said. "Wrapping lemon wedges in cheesecloth. I saw that on a show about a fancy restaurant in Europe one time, how they wrap lemon wedges there in this really nice cheesecloth, so that people never get seeds in the stuff they squeeze fresh lemons on. Anyway, I thought that was a great idea."

"Oh."

I kept fishing. "Yeah."

"Kenny Jenkins would be run out of Blue Creek for doing something like putting cheesecloth on lemons," Bahar said.

Behind the counter, Kenny Jenkins's ears perked up. I'm sure he'd caught mention of his name. He glared at me. I looked at my tea, wondering if he even knew that his son was coming back to Blue Creek that day.

Bahar sighed. "Anyway, it's pretty sad."

"What is? That A. C. Messer turned out to be a—excuse me—jerk?"

She smiled again. Air.

Bahar said, "Well, yeah. That was pretty sad. But I was talking about you, how you're leaving Blue Creek. It'll be different here without you."

"Yeah. What will Blue Creek be without the Little Boy in the Haunted Well?"

"You must be so excited."

Now the spiders were running laps, beating drums, setting off fireworks, and playing lawn darts.[82]

"I . . . Um . . ."

"You have to promise to text me as soon as you get settled in at your school, Sam." My cell phone sat on the table next to my tea. Bahar touched it with an index finger.

I shook my head. "They don't allow kids to have cell phones there."

Bahar's eyes widened like one of Mr. Blank's *babies*. She said, "No cell phones? That's as uncivilized as unsweetened tea in Texas."

And that made me laugh, but I also felt my eyes getting a little puffy and steamy, too, and what the (excuse me) heck was happening to me?

I said, "I'm going to be lonely. I'm going to . . . miss you, Bahar."

I still hadn't given up on trying to snag that lemon seed with my straw, even though I was failing miserably. Then Bahar did something that instantaneously knocked all the spiders

---

[82] Lawn darts is a very dangerous game where people throw heavy, sharp things really high up in the air and try to get them to stick into the ground in the center of a hoop. It's kind of like cornhole, except you could die.

into a collective state of unconsciousness. She reached across the table and grabbed my hand.

We held hands.

And she said, "I'll miss you, Sam. It won't be bad, though. And you *won't* be lonely, trust me. I know you, Sam Abernathy. Besides, you'll come home for holidays and stuff, right?"

I couldn't even talk. All I could think about was Bahar's hand holding mine, and my hand holding hers back, how weird and magic it felt, and how I no longer cared about that (excuse me) dumb lemon seed swimming around in the iced tea I was having such a hard time tasting. And then I noticed that Kenny Jenkins was staring at us, watching us holding hands, and I felt myself getting hot and turning red.

My phone buzzed and rotated a thin sliver of an arc on the tabletop.

There was a text message from James Jenkins: **Just got to Blue Creek. Still looks the same, sadly enough** 😂**. We'll be at your house in about 5 minutes. Can't wait!!!**

MY FRIEND JAMES

Anyone who'd ever met James Jenkins would have mar-veled at how much he had changed in the few months since I'd last seen him.

He looked older and leaner, almost like he hadn't been eating enough. His football body had smoothed out into something straighter and taller, and you could sense a kind of confidence and even happiness in him just in seeing the way he stood and how he moved.

James and his mom got to my house before I did.

His mother, Linda Swineshead, was already gone by the time I showed up. It was a relief. I didn't know if I could face James's mother after finding out that she had been my dad's *girlfriend* at one time. That was one part of the whole Purdy House history and experience I don't think I'll ever get rid of.

And I was late because Bahar and I may or may not have walked back from the diner through Lake Marion Park, where we possibly had taken off our shoes and socks and waded in the water for one last time before we might have stopped off so I could hypothetically say a final good-bye to Sam's Well before walking Bahar to her door, all of which, if in fact it happened, made me just a little bit too late to greet my friend and his mom when they arrived at my house.

Anyway, James just smiled at me with a sneaky expression when he saw me. He didn't say anything. He didn't have to. I knew he was going to tease me because of the awkward response I'd made to the text message he'd sent when I was at Colonel Jenkins's Diner. Because I said this: I'll be right there. I'm just saying good-bye to Bahar.

They should make phones with some kind of vacuum-cleaner feature, so you can suck back texts that you realize tell more than you want to, but then it's too late because you already hit send and put them out into the universe, and you know your friend is going to tease you because YOU DO NOT HAVE A CRUSH ON BAHAR. Or whoever.

James didn't have any shoes on his feet. He was eating watermelon in the kitchen with Mom, Dad, Dylan, and Evie when I walked in.

James Jenkins wiped his mouth with the back of a hand and said, "It's about time you showed up, Sam!"

Then he moved toward me very slowly (James, as I have said in the past, was known for walking extremely slowly), like he was stepping on broken glass.

"Oh my gosh! What's wrong?" I said.

"Nothing. I just tore my feet up at the academy. I can't even put regular shoes on," James said.

Then he kind of grimaced when he took another two steps toward me and then put his arms around me and hugged me hard. It was weird because I had never hugged James Jenkins before, but it felt good and I found myself feeling sad, too, because I was thinking about all those things I'd done growing up in Blue Creek—and all those things I had to say good-bye to. There was a part of my life when I used to be so terrified of James Jenkins too, when I would have believed that he might crush my spine in his monstrous grab. And it was weird because the top of my head barely reached James's chin (because James Jenkins was giant, and monstrous, but he also loved to dance, which made James as rare and as irreplaceable as anyone I'd ever known). Besides, James kind of smelled bad, which is exactly what you'd expect of a teenage boy who'd been sitting inside a car, driving through Texas on a hot summer day.

And James said, "You grew about a foot!"

Well, that was nice of James, but Mom and Dad kept tabs. I was exactly three quarters of an inch taller than when school had started last fall. I said, "Yeah. And you're a giraffe."

And I couldn't help but imagine what a stuffed giraffe would look like inside the Purdy House.

Karim ended up coming back from the library in the evening, when we were all about to sit down for dinner. He and Brenden

Saltarello must have patched things up after Brenden discovered the new (artificial) common ground they shared over Princess Snugglewarm.

It worked out for me, because it gave me a chance to talk to James Jenkins alone—so I could clue him in on what NOT to say out loud in front of Karim, which basically meant anything having to do with his cousin Bahar, or the general topics of crushes and such.

"Gosh! Middle school kids are so goofy about stuff," James said. James Jenkins was going to start tenth grade this year, so he knew almost everything.

We'd been hiding in my room from the rest of my family, playing video games and looking at books.

"I wouldn't know. I never spent much time there," I said. "Besides, I may be twelve, but I'm about to start ninth grade, so that automatically puts me ahead of the game."

And just saying that activated all the spiders and set them into a frenzy like angry bears unpleasantly awakened from hibernation.

James just said, "Hmmf," which is the way James Jenkins laughed if he thought something was really funny. Then he said, "Anyway, I just needed to say thank you for talking me out of quitting dance when I wanted to."

"I didn't do anything," I said.

"You did a lot more than anyone else did. I don't even have any friends at all because of my dad, and football, and now after leaving Blue Creek. You're my only real friend. Do you even realize how many friends you have?"

I guess I'd never really thought about it like that.

And James went on, "After leaving Blue Creek and quitting football, it's like I was erased or something. Like I'm blank."

Blank.

"That reminds me," I said. "I've got a cool story for you about a haunted house, and a weird family of people who may or may not be monsters, and you know what their name is? Their name is 'Blank.'"

"Hmmf," James said.

We sat there in my room, just saying nothing, which is what friends do a lot of times. I heard James flipping pages in the book he was looking through. It was *Children of Dune*. We'd both read it a long time ago. Duh. Who wouldn't read a book like that?

I had actually moved on to my second summer reading novel. And now I was beginning to think I'd get things done in time for the new school year, and moving away, and all that other stuff.

The light was turning to evening-shade. I could hear Mom in the kitchen. She was probably making something for dinner that would call for some expert help, but I was too busy doing nothing with James.

Finally he said, "Well? Are you going to tell me about the haunted house or what?"

"Yeah," I said. "Yeah. But I just wanted to ask you something first. I don't know if you can help me or not, but I thought since you're about to start tenth grade and stuff . . . Um. It's about having a crush on someone."

"Hmmf."

BYE-BYE, BLUE CREEK

No one likes good-byes.

It took us three days to drive from Blue Creek to Albuquerque, where James's mom was waiting for him. Dad said there were so many amazing things we needed to see on our way. So we visited the world's largest fruitcake (which was shaped like Texas and weighed one hundred fifty pounds), the Billy the Kid Museum, and the world's largest roadrunner[83] in Fort Stockton. Before we got to Albuquerque, we also stopped off at the world's largest pistachio.

There were so many of the world's largest things in between Blue Creek and New Mexico that you would think North America might sink into the ocean under all that size and weight. Also, the giant pistachio made me want to cook something daring, like lemon-pistachio pasta, only not with a pistachio the size of Dad's car.

Karim moved back into his house. After all, there was

---

[83] His name is Paisano Pete, and he isn't a real roadrunner, and he is also not the world's largest, but we saw him anyway. Then we saw the actual "world's largest roadrunner," which was in New Mexico.

nowhere left for him to go once everything had been packed up and I was finally ready to take all my spiders away with me to school in Oregon. Mom and Dad sent him off with wishes that his parents had fully recovered from the devastation of the nudist-camp sunburns they'd gotten from a vacation in Mexico that had never happened. In true Karim form, he'd said, "Thanks, Mr. and Mrs. Abernathy. They'll be fine once the doctors wake them up from their medically induced comas. Until then, I have to feed them jarred baby food!"

And Mom had said, "Oh, Karim! That sounds dreadful!"

But Karim had just shrugged and said, "It's no big deal. It happens every summer."

I felt a little bit guilty for being an accomplice in fooling Brenden Saltarello into rethinking his relationship with Karim. I gave Karim my Princess Snugglewarm T-shirt and pajamas to keep while I was away at Pine Mountain Academy. I didn't check, but I was pretty sure the school (or the students, at the very least) wouldn't approve if I brought them with me. Anyway, Brenden was a good guy. If I ever open a restaurant in Blue Creek, I'll ask him if he wants a job as maître d'.[84]

But that last time I walked with Karim back to his house and we each carried a bundle of the things that used to be mine but were now his,[85] my heart felt heavier than any giant pista-

---

[84] Which is a fancy word for "headwaiter," the equivalent of putting cheesecloth on lemon wedges in Blue Creek.

[85] Even though Karim insisted he was only going to do laundry for me— that it was the least he could do for wearing my clothes all summer long.

ANDREW SMITH

chio or roadrunner that ever stood as false evidence to their size or their truth.

I was unprepared for it.

We both just stood there on his front porch and stared at the door. I could hear the television inside Karim's house. His parents, who were not in medically induced comas and had never gone to Mexico, were watching a game show, probably enjoying the freedom and peace of summer.

"Oh, well, I guess this is good-bye," Karim said.

"Um . . . I could help you carry this stuff inside," I said.

"You don't have to. Besides, my parents might not recognize me and then call the police on us."

That probably wasn't a lie, I thought.

"Karim . . . I've never *not* known you for my entire life," I said. My voice was quivery, and I felt a little embarrassed.

"Well, I know you wouldn't call the cops on me, Sam."

But Karim wouldn't look at me. He turned away and sniffled, and then he put his bundle of clothes down on the wooden swing and wiped an arm across the bottom of his nose. This shouldn't have been happening. I had never—not once in my life—seen my best friend sad like this, and if he started to cry, I knew I was going to cry too, and then we'd be two dumb[86] kids bawling on a porch on a hot summer day in Texas while I was holding on to a bunch of pajamas and stuff. Nobody wants to see that.

---

[86] (excuse me)

"Because you'll never *not* be my best friend, Sam," Karim said.

"Okay."

"Yeah. So. You'd better go now."

"I guess."

I piled my bundle of clothes beside the ones Karim had left on his swing.

Karim said, "No going into haunted houses without me."

"It's a deal."

Then Karim hugged me, and we both got so mad at ourselves because we had to wait out there on his dumb[87] porch until we stopped crying. And when he went inside, he said, "If my parents notice anything, I'm going to tell them you slapped me."

"It's a deal."

Bahar had written a note to me, which she'd folded up and tucked into one of the pockets of my official Pine Mountain Academy duffel bag. She'd asked me not to read it until I got to Oregon, but I opened it before we even saw the giant fruitcake. She had written it on the back of my gooseneck-barnacles home-chef-services flyer from the Teen Zone at the Blue Creek Public Library.

I guess there was no sense in leaving that up in Blue Creek anymore.

---

[87] (excuse me)

ANDREW SMITH

The note said this:

The first Saturday you're back, let's have iced tea and
make Kenny Jenkins mad!
—Love, B

Look, it's always okay to sign a note to a friend with "Love."
It DOES NOT mean you have a crush or anything.

So eventually the Blank family and their excessively
unpleasant child, Boris, would turn the Purdy House into a
mechanized bedlam of an amusement park, complete with
their Little Boy in the Haunted Well attraction, and Dad, taking every advantage of the increase in tourists coming to Blue
Creek, would begin putting up hand-painted road signs along
the interstate that advertised THE WORLD'S BIGGEST MECHA-
NIZED LLAMA as well as his new side business, which was Blue
Creek Kilts.

And once all the floods of sunburned travelers began pour-
ing into Blue Creek, looking for the most haunted house in
all of Texas (and the world's biggest mechanized llama), everything was bound to change, and James Jenkins, Bahar, Karim,
and all the rest of Blue Creek and I wouldn't be the only ones
who had to say the world's biggest good-bye.